POLICEMAN'S PROGRESS

A Sixties Mystery

BERNARD KNIGHT

First published in Great Britain by Robert Hale Ltd 1969
This edition published by Accent Press 2016

ISBN 9781910939932

To all my CID friends in the North-East, and especially to the River Tyne Police, hoping they will not mind my overruling the Home Secretary in creating a 'Tyneside Constabulary' for the purposes of this book!

Author's note

The Sixties Mysteries is a series of reissues of my early crime stories, the first of which was originally published in 1963. Looking back now, it is evident how criminal investigation has changed over the last half-century. Though basic police procedure is broadly the same, in these pages you will find no Crime Scene Managers or Crown Prosecution Service, no DNA, CSI, PACE, nor any of the other acronyms beloved of modern novels and television. These were the days when detectives still wore belted raincoats and trilby hats. There was no Health and Safety to plague us and the police smoked and drank tea alongside the post-mortem table!

Modern juries are now more interested in the reports of the forensic laboratory than in the diligent labours of the humble detective, though it is still the latter that solves most serious crimes. This is not to by any means belittle the enormous advances made in forensic science in recent years, but to serve as a reminder that the old murder teams did a pretty good job based simply on experience and dogged investigation.

Bernard Knight
2015

Chapter One

The launch squatted with its stern well down in the icy water, a long wake bubbling behind. With its black hull and dark varnished cabin, it was almost invisible. Only the navigation lights gleamed against the river.

'Too damned cold for crime tonight, Horace!'

The sergeant's words condensed into puffs of mist as they left his lips. In spite of the radiator alongside his seat, it was freezing in the cabin, which was open to the sky at the back end.

'Must be a coupla degrees o' frost tonight,' he said again.

The constable in the driving seat alongside made a gargling noise in reply. The sergeant sighed. It was hard work trying to be sociable with Horace.

For a few moments he sat staring through the windscreen at the deep gorge of the Tyne, as it cut through between Newcastle and Gateshead. They were approaching the narrowest part, where three bridges crowded together to form the road links from Northumberland to Durham, and just passing the River Police Station for this section of the Tyne, but the launch throbbed on, and swept under the graceful arch of the huge Tyne Bridge to pass into the more open water beyond, with no other bridge between them and the sea, eight miles away.

The sergeant's eyes roved the quaysides, only to see nothing but frosted cranes and deserted streets.

'Quiet, isn't it?' he said, with no hope of response from the taciturn driver.

Then he glimpsed a moving red light in the distance, where the river took a bend to the right.

'Hopper's coming up, Horace,' he said, trying to prod his constable into saying something, even if it was only 'Belt up!' But the other man kept his jaw clamped shut and spun the wheel over to keep the launch well clear of the *Bessie Surtees* as she came pounding up towards them. The *Bessie* was one of the power station hoppers, condemned to her eternal task of humping boiler ash down to its grave in the open sea.

The wake of the hopper hit them after she passed and Horace jammed the brass throttle lever back to 'Half Speed' as they bounced like a cork in a bucket. The mournful hoot of the *Bessie*'s siren echoed over the sleeping city as she signalled the Swing Bridge.

As the sound died away, the sergeant jabbed a finger in the direction of the north bank. 'Let's go and have a squint at Jackie Stott's old hulk,' he commanded hopefully. Things were far too quiet for Ernie Leadbitter's taste – any diversion would be welcome on a blank shift like this one.

Horace shoved the throttle back to 'Full' and the thirty-two foot launch cleaved her way through the black water towards the Newcastle bank. Their destination, contemptuously called an 'old hulk' by the sergeant, was a converted torpedo boat. Stripped of engines and, in fact, almost everything else except the actual hull, it was now re-named the *Mississippi*. Owned by Jackie Stott, a local nightclub proprietor, it had been turned into a floating gaming casino and moored on a particularly dismal stretch of the riverside.

It was one of the ambitions of the Tyneside Constabulary to pin something on Jackie but, so far, the wily ex-boxer had been too slippery for them. There was a healthy rivalry between Central Division, which covered his club in the city centre, and the River Police, who had jurisdiction over the floating part of Stott's empire.

Ernie Leadbitter had long cherished the hope of catching Jackie or one of his minions at some piece of evil, even if it was only an infringement of the gaming or licensing laws.

'If only that bloody barge would go adrift, I could even nick him for failure to show lights!' he hollered at Horace, as the launch closed with the *Mississippi*.

Horace burst into a rare flow of eloquence. 'Have a job to get Jackie for owt to do with the watter,' he grunted in his ripe Geordie accent. 'He spent the war on them MTBs. Knows his way about the sea, does Jackie.'

Leadbitter looked sourly at the dirty white hull of the torpedo boat, reflected in the street lights of the quayside. 'That's why he bought this abomination, I suppose – sentimental value!'

Horace guffawed. 'Jackie's aboot as sentimental as a bull elephant … though he must like boats, I'll grant. He's got that canny twin-screw launch moored up at Scotswood … only bought her back in the spring.'

'Must be making a packet outta these mugs on the gaming tables,' muttered Leadbitter resentfully, staring across the water at one of Stott's sources of wealth.

As they came nearer, Horace cut the diesel to neutral and they glided in a smooth curve to where the *Mississippi* lay moored. The old war boat had been stripped of all her deck fittings. The only superstructure was a glorified garden shed with a door, but no windows. A single string of coloured bulbs hung over the gangway which, at this state of the tide, was almost horizontal.

'Looks quiet – they can't be doing much business,' said Ernie with regret.

'Heard tell they're dee'in aalreet – rough crowd and all get down here. The more respectable clients go up to the Rising Sun.'

The police launch was almost alongside the old MTB now, gliding up to her starboard quarter. Ernie got off the padded seat and walked back to the open deck alongside the engine casing, ready to step up onto the gunwale. He looked up at the bulk of the *Mississippi*, then stiffened as his ears picked up some noise. He stuck his head back under the cabin roof.

'Kill the engine – quick!' he hissed.

As the tickover of the Perkins engine died away, Leadbitter hopped up on the gunwale, then leaned out and grabbed one of the stanchions that carried the rail around the edge of the torpedo boat.

The police launch stopped her forward glide and Horace's face appeared below him. For once, the sergeant wanted him to keep quiet. He made a 'shhh' sign and the constable saw him jerk a thumb in the direction of the other craft's gangway.

They both listened.

Horace could see nothing from below, but he could hear a thumping, scuffling sound, then voices.

'Gerroff, yer ugly great bleeder. I'm on the level, I tell yer!'

'Shurrup! If the boss says "get", you gets, see!'

There was a skidding, rattling and grunting – Leadbitter, with his eyes just above deck level, saw two figures struggling under the line of coloured bulbs. The gangway was wobbling violently as the larger of two figures wrestled and buffeted the smaller towards the quayside.

The cursing and panting increased, then one of the men collapsed, the top half of his body sticking perilously over the edge of the gangway. His assailant began kicking his side and buttocks with apparent relish.

The sergeant decided that things had gone far enough. He hauled himself up by the stanchion and ducked beneath the rail, followed by Horace.

For the first time, the two men on the gangway were aware of the arrival of the police. The big one saw

Leadbitter first. He stopped battering the other man, then quickly bent down and heaved him to his feet. Incongruously, he began brushing him down with a hand the size of a ham.

'What d'you think you're at, Joe?' snapped Leadbitter. 'Come on, let's be having you both back on the deck here.'

Amiable and gentle most of the time, Sergeant Leadbitter was a different man when dealing with villains. He was a heavily built fellow and had an 'official' voice with a real bite of authority in it.

Joe Blunt, the one who had been doing the kicking, sullenly came off the gangway, dragging his victim behind him.

Neither of them spoke, but both eyed the police officers with a mixture of truculence and apprehension. The smaller man, sandy-haired and in his late twenties, seemed not a bit grateful for his deliverance. He glowered at the sergeant every bit as resentfully as Joe, who was a great hulking figure with a piggy, moronic face, beaten out of shape by years of third-class boxing.

Ernie peered more closely at the smaller fellow, who was sulkily twisting his rumpled dinner jacket back into shape. 'I know you, don't I?' he demanded.

'He's Geordie Armstrong – spins the wheel for Jackie Stott,' volunteered Horace.

The policemen looked expectantly at the big bruiser.

'Well?' Ernie sounded impatient.

'It was nothing … jus' a bit o' fun, you know,' rumbled Joe Blunt eventually.

Leadbitter snorted derisively. 'Fun be damned! You were kicking the hell outta his backside a minute past. Come on, don't give me that!'

'Only a bit of a lark … I'm not complaining about 'im,' muttered Geordie Armstrong.

'Joe's gone back into the sparring partner business, has he!' Horace laid the sarcasm on thickly. 'You paying a

5

coupla bob for a practice bout, Geordie, that it?'

'Very bloody funny,' snarled Armstrong, showing his teeth. 'I tell you it was nothing. So shove off, will yer!'

'Yes, this is a private patch, this … you got no call to be 'ere,' rumbled Joe Blunt, taking a lead from his former victim.

Ernie Leadbitter stepped close to the punchy old 'pro'. He was not quite as big, but he had a steely glint in his eye that made the loose-lipped face turn away. 'Watch your tongue, Joe … any sort of disturbance on this converted muck barge is our business.' He turned and grasped Joe's arm. 'Come on, let's get below … is your gaffer in?'

Joe, thoroughly cowed by the sergeant's vibrant authority, turned to shamble back to the door in the clumsy superstructure of the *Mississippi*. Geordie was more belligerent and angrily shook off Horace as the constable reached out to steer him after Joe Blunt. The boxer opened the door, which carried a notice stating *Members Only*, and stepped into a carpeted entrance which had a flight of stairs running down immediately to their left.

At the head of the stairs, Joe made a last stand. 'I tell you, we was only having a bit o' fun – the boss will do me for letting you in here,' he pleaded.

'And *I'll* do you if you don't – so get on!' snapped Ernie.

Looking like a dejected hippopotamus, Joe tramped down the stairs, leading the others into the big single room of the casino. It occupied three-quarters of the hull, as a cloakroom filled the pointed bow and the stern was partitioned off into an office. A bar ran along one side, the rest of the place being filled with roulette, blackjack and *chemin de fer* tables. There were about twenty-five men in the room and the moment the police uniforms appeared at the foot of the stairs, a deathly hush fell on the place.

Faces were raised and cards were held against chests. The click of the roulette ball went on unheeded for a few seconds while the procession headed for the door of Jackie Stott's office. Joe tapped and went in. Geordie Armstrong crowded in after Joe, aided by a helpful push in the back from Horace.

A bull-like voice bellowed out before the policemen could enter.

'What in hell are you doing back ... didn't I tell you to duff him up a bit, Joe!'

There was the thump of clenched fist on a desk and Geordie cringed back against the constable. Suddenly, the speaker caught sight of the police uniforms and bit his words off in mid-air.

'What the hell's this, then?' Like Joe and Geordie, he had a broad Tyneside accent.

The officers pushed through the door and saw Jackie Stott standing behind his desk, glowering at them. The room seemed full of big men. Geordie, who would not have been out of place in a group of average-sized people, was dwarfed. Joe and the two policemen were all six-foot-plus, with shoulders to match. Jackie Stott was in the same class. He was younger, in his early forties, and coarsely handsome, though a repeatedly broken nose marred his looks. Straw-coloured hair was waved in tight furrows close to his bullet head. His pale blue eyes were sharp and knowing – he'd had the sense to get out of the professional ring long before he had become a punchy wreck like Joe Blunt, his old sparring partner.

Stott stared suspiciously at Horace and Leadbitter, whom he knew well by sight.

'What's it this time – you coppers trying to nick me for something again?'

'We're not trying anything,' answered Leadbitter, untruthfully. 'We're just seeing that everyone sticks to the rules, Jackie.'

'Like hell you are – and I'm *Mr Stott* to you, copper.'

Ernie smiled gently. 'You were Jackie to us fifteen

years ago, when we used to see you hammer the champions up at St James' Hall – so Jackie will do for me now.'

Stott was appeased at once. The wily sergeant knew when to use a bit of 'soft soap'.

'So what's all the fuss?' he asked in a more moderate voice. 'Are we sinking or has our liquor licence expired?'

Leadbitter waved at Joe and Geordie. 'Assault – creating a disturbance – breaking the peace … Joe hammering the daylights outta Geordie here. Know anything about it?'

Stott glared at Joe Blunt and the great oaf looked as if he was going to burst into tears.

Jackie looked back at the policemen. 'Don't ask me … but you know Joe here, he's a bit soft in the head. No accounting what he'll get up to.' He snapped back at his henchman, 'What you bin doing, you great clart?'

Joe's limping brain could hardly keep up with the turn of events.

'Well, you told me to …'

'Shurrup!' cut in Jackie, quickly. 'What's it all about, Geordie?' His eyes bored into the young man's with such venomous warning, that Geordie got the message without difficulty.

He gulped. 'Jus' me an' Joe having a bit o' fun, you know.'

Leadbitter snorted. 'The hell you were! Think I'm daft? Joe here had you down on the deck, putting the boot in.'

Both Joe and Geordie made loud, if unconvincing, denials until Jackie cut them off short.

'Look, you damn fools, if you want horseplay, you go down to the gym in the morning, not foul up my boat, kicking up a row.' He turned to the sergeant. 'Sorry, sarge, but like I said, Joe's a few ounces short when it comes to brains.'

Leadbitter sighed. 'Do me a favour, Jackie … when I

came in just now, I heard you mention a "duffing up" – so did the constable here. Brawling in public is an offence and I want to know why I shouldn't book Joe here for disorderly behaviour, if not something worse.'

'Geordie's making no charge – are you, Geordie?' snapped Stott, throwing a flaming look at the unfortunate George Armstrong. 'And it was on the boat, which is private property. Not in the street or quayside, so why not drop it, eh?'

Ernie looked piercingly at Armstrong. '*Are* you making any complaint, Geordie? I know damn well that Joe was giving you the bum's rush. What's it all about?'

The young man looked fearfully at his employer, not at the police. 'I'm making no charge, like Mr Stott says … it was all a bit o' fun.'

Leadbitter grunted. He could make a case of it, he supposed, but was it worth it? It was private property, but in full public view. The fact that Geordie made no complaint was irrelevant in the case of a public nuisance. But he was sorry for the pathetic punch-drunk old boxer, and it was he who would be the only one to suffer if there were a prosecution. He had several previous convictions for violence – as had his boss, Jackie – and he would be sure to get a prison sentence with his record. Jackie was the one behind it and he would get off unscathed. Ernie decided it was better to add the information to their store against Stott, rather than victimise his strong-arm man.

'I'll have to report it in and see what action needs to be taken,' he said rather pompously. 'Let's have no more messing about tonight – or any other night. You've got a licence to think of, Jackie, as we both well know. There's lots of folks who'd be glad to see this hulk cleared off the river – and I'm one of 'em.'

He turned on his heel and walked out, Horace close behind. They walked through another zone of silence in the gaming room and up onto the deck.

Geordie Armstrong scuttled along close behind and vanished over the gangway before any more misfortune could overtake him.

Before Joe had lumbered out of the deck house, the officers were climbing down into their launch.

'Watch it, Joe – keep your nose clean,' called up Leadbitter as Horace cast off. 'With the form you've got, you can't afford to be up before the beaks too often.'

The diesel roared again as Horace pulled away from the *Mississippi*. The sergeant took the radio handset from a cubby hole and called up Control in distant South Shields.

'Tyne Pol Control, *D for Dog* here, *D for Dog*. Resuming patrol after being off the air at the Ouseburn … any messages?'

A crackled negative reassured Ernie. He sat hunched in his seat alongside the stolid Horace and wondered what the hell the performance on Jackie's boat had *really* been about.

Chapter Two

Back on the *Mississippi*, Jackie Stott was tearing into his henchman, who ineffectually tried to defend himself.

''Ow the 'ell was I to know there was a bloody copper looking over me shoulder?'

'I didn't tell you to half-kill him in full view of all Newcastle, did I?' snarled Jackie. 'I should 'a left you to go to a mental home, where you belong, Joe, instead of trying to look after you! My good nature will be the death of me one day.'

Joe Blunt looked like a faithful spaniel who had just collected a kick in the ribs from its master. 'I'm sorry, honest … but Geordie tried to cut up rough after you told me to chuck him ashore.'

'You never miss a chance to thump Geordie, do you, Joe!'

Stott stubbed his cigarette out angrily and snatched a camel-hair coat from the back of the door.

As Joe hurried to help him into it, he said, 'I'm going through to the Bigg Market – I've got to talk to Thor Hansen about this business of Geordie.'

The club owner marched to the door and made a last plea before he opened it.

'Now for God's sake, try to keep out of trouble for the rest of the flaming night – you know the police are dying to get the drop on me for something.'

He hurried through the gaming room, giving nods to many of the regular patrons as he went. Joe lumbered after him, muttering promises of good behaviour, until he vanished over the gangway.

A few minutes later, Stott reached the city centre in his white Mercedes, stopping at a now sleeping parking meter in the cobbled area of the Bigg Market.

The Rising Sun Club occupied two floors above a furniture shop. The premises were narrow but deep, squeezed in between a public house and a tiny lane which led to a court containing another pub and the back entrance of a large multiple store.

Jackie strode up to the narrow entrance of the club with a proprietary swagger and ran up the steep stairs easily – though starting to run to fat, he was still a very powerful man. Over-eating and over-drinking had not yet made too many inroads into his strength and virility.

At the top was another door into a small foyer, where two small rooms were partitioned off. The first cubicle did duty both as cloakroom and sentry box.

'Evening, sir.'

A tall, thin man with a harelip jumped up from a stool behind the cloakroom counter. This was Herbert Lumley, an old soldier who acted as doorman, cloakroom attendant and chucker-out.

Jackie grunted at him. 'Where's Hansen, Herb?'

'I believe the manager is upstairs, sir – I saw him with Miss Laura a few minutes past.'

The straight-backed old fellow was a stickler for propriety. Once a sergeant in the Northumberland Fusiliers, he seemed out of place in a nightclub, until one saw him ejecting a bunch of troublemakers with a calm efficiency that showed the strength of both his character and his muscles.

Jackie pushed through the inner doors to meet a blast of warm air and the throb of a four-piece group on the low stage.

The big room on the first floor was given over to drinking, cabaret and dancing, in that order of importance. It was after Laura Levine's first singing spot of the evening, but too early for the strip show.

Turning left, Jackie went up a second flight of stairs to the top floor. Here, another glass door led into the casino, but alongside it was a plain door fitted with a Chubb lock. This was his own flat, which shared the second floor with the gaming part of his establishment. There was even a secret peephole from his lounge into the casino, so that he could keep a personal eye on things.

As Stott let himself in, he heard a woman's voice from the lounge.

He pushed open the lounge door and nodded at the two occupants. They were sitting as far apart as the room would allow, but only since his key had been heard in the lock.

'Hi, Laura ... hello, Thor. Let's have a drink.'

He slumped down on to the settee and his big hand dropped possessively onto the woman's thigh. He squeezed and she smiled mechanically at him.

'How's the *Mississippi* ... much of a crowd tonight?' Thor Hansen's slight Danish accent contrasted with Jackie's local one.

'Crowd's fair enough – but that blasted Geordie Armstrong is screwing it up for me!'

He half-turned and shot a queer look at Laura Levine, as if expecting some reaction from her. She looked back blankly at him from under her false black lashes and he buried his nose in the glass that Hansen handed him.

Thor brought another drink for the woman, then sat opposite with his own. 'I told you he needed watching ... better have him back up here, where we can keep an eye on him.'

Jackie snorted. 'You may be needing a bloody magnifying glass to keep an eye on him, one of these days.'

'What d'you mean?' snapped Laura.

'I mean that I'll be tearing Geordie into little bits if I

definitely catch him out.' Again he gave her a suspicious look. Thor's calculating eyes watched them both.

'What's Geordie been up to, then?' She spoke nonchalantly, crossing her legs to escape Jackie's caress.

He scowled at her. 'Don't you know?'

She ignored him and the Dane covered up the awkward moment with a question. 'Joe has been making trouble, I guess?'

Stott threw down his whisky in one gulp and held out his glass for another. 'Aye, Joe Blunt hates his guts all right. Tried to kick him into the Tyne tonight – in full view of the coppers, silly oaf!'

Thor Hansen's blond eyebrows rose. He was a typical handsome Scandinavian; tall, slim, with a longish face and crisp fair hair.

'Geordie's been fiddling the wheel somehow,' went on Stott, 'I can't figure out how he's doing it and I can't catch him at it, blast him!'

'Are his takings down every night?'

'Just a fraction – he's not fool enough to try to twist the house much, but he's soaking the mugs somehow, I'll swear. I know the signs – a coupla new suits, bought himself a nearly new Cortina. Where the hell's he gettin' it, if he ain't twisting the table?'

Laura Levine stretched herself back against the corner of the settee and curled her feet under her.

'Perhaps he's knocked over a bank or a wages van,' she said languidly.

'Very bloody funny!' snapped Jackie. 'He couldn't knock over a blind beggar and steal his tin! Playing the wheel is all he's got talent for – that and chasing birds,' he added ominously. He glared at Laura again. 'And another thing – has he been hanging around here, while I've been away in Middlesbrough?'

Thor's face went blank and he stared at the opposite wall, but Laura came to life with a rush.

14

'What the hell are you getting at, Jackie?' she snapped furiously. 'Ever since you came in, you've been insinuating something … are you going punchy, the same way as Joe Blunt?'

'Look here, you bitch …'

'Don't you "bitch" me, Jackie Stott!' she spat. 'If you're trying to make out that Geordie Armstrong and me are having it off, you must be off your bloody rocker. You're bad enough, but *him*!'

'Look, lay off or I'll fetch you one around the ear!' yelled the furious Jackie.

By way of reply, Laura pulled off one of her shoes and tried to hit him in the face with the stiletto heel. He parried it easily and slapped her face with a force that almost unhinged her head.

Thor sat with a pale, composed face while the other two fought, each pouring a steady stream of abuse at the other. The Dane was used to such scenes and, much as he disliked them, he had the sense to wait his opportunity without interfering.

This one was shorter than usual. The girl pulled away and stood barefooted, panting and enraged. She tried to straighten her dress and pushed her genuinely red hair back from her face.

'You bastard – you've done that once too often,' she gasped. 'Look at the damned mess you've made of me and I've got my second number in a couple of minutes!'

Jackie grinned up at her from the settee, his bad humour gone. He had obviously enjoyed the fight, getting some mildly sadistic pleasure from it. 'That's my girl – red hair and green eyes! Go and get yourself a new dress tomorrow and charge it to me.'

'Stuff your dress!' she flared, pulling on her shoes. 'I'm sleeping at my place tonight and don't you damn well try to come around there.'

She stalked to the door leading to the bathroom and

slammed it behind her.

Jackie leered at Thor Hansen. 'I like a bit of spirit. I tell you, son, she's tops at everything, not only singing … if I wasn't already married, I wouldn't mind making it legal one of these days.'

As his wife had deserted him ten years ago, this wouldn't have been much of a problem to Jackie, but he had never bothered. Until recently, Laura either spent her nights at the flat in the Rising Sun or else Jackie went to the flat he had provided her with in Gosforth, just outside the city.

Thor had his own ideas about Laura and her accomplishments, but again he was wise enough to keep them well to himself. 'What about this Geordie Armstrong business?' he asked now.

He was a businessman through and through – anything that touched the profits of the clubs might eventually touch him, if things went as he planned. He was officially Jackie's manager at the Rising Sun, but Stott leaned heavily on his know-how and advice for all his legitimate businesses. As well as this place in the Bigg Market, he had the *Mississippi*, a couple of betting shops in outlying towns and, on Hansen's initiative, was just about to open a new and bigger nightclub at Middlesbrough.

Jackie tore his mind from thoughts of Laura's body. 'I'll get Geordie myself – this time, I don't need your help. He came from the gutter and that's where he'll damn well end up. I'd have given him the push tonight, only you know as well as I do that good croupiers are hard to come by – and Geordie is a good one, when he plays it straight.'

Hansen considered this for a moment. 'If his pay-in is all right, why are you so dead against him? He can't be cheating us, if he's getting the normal rake-off for the house.'

Jackie's bad humour began to gather again. 'I just got a hunch! He may not be fiddling us direct, but somehow he's skinning the mugs to his own advantage.' He prodded the air with a finger the size of a sausage. 'If we get, say sixty per cent of the cash the mugs bring in with them, then they share the other forty between them … that's OK. But if another ten per cent is being switched into Geordie's pocket, that's bad business for us.'

'But to do that, he'd have to have a partner hidden amongst the patrons.' Hansen was too proper to use the word 'mugs'.

Jackie nodded. 'S'right! … and when I catch him, I'll wrap his face around these.' He held up a handful of great knuckles. 'And the other hand will be for Geordie. If he's got any sense, he'll drop any funny business right now.' He took another mouthful of neat whiskey. 'But that's not all – I think the little swine is after my Laura.'

Thor's deadpan expression stayed put, while he faced Jackie, but as he turned to put down his glass, a fleeting smile crossed his face.

'I was in her flat a week last Friday,' went on the club owner. 'There was an ashtray half full of fag ends. You know she never smokes, says it's bad for her voice.'

Thor kept his voice level, but unconsciously stubbed out his own half-finished cigarette.

'Nothing in that, for heaven's sake.'

Stott prowled around the room.

'Suppose not – but it never happened before. For a couple of months past, she's been coming the iceberg with me. If we got together a couple of nights a week, I was lucky. This last fortnight, I haven't had so much as a tickle … she's always got some tale about being tired or ill or going out or summat!'

'What's this got to do with Geordie Armstrong?'

Jackie's face blackened like a thundercloud.

'Joe Blunt says he's heard tales around the pubs … Geordie hinting – boasting like – that he's shacked up with some fabulous bird. In the boozer last night Joe heard him tell someone that he'd be surprised if I knew who it was.'

Thor shrugged. 'You can't believe a word Joe says – apart from being punch-drunk, he'd lie his head off to get Geordie into trouble.'

Stott shook his head angrily.

'I still got a hunch, you know.' His accent thickened as he got excited and Hansen was hard pressed to understand him at times. 'Laura's been my bird over two years now. She hadn't a bean when I gave her this singing job – now she's got a car, her own flat, as much cash as she wants. Perhaps I aren't Richard Burton and Gregory Peck rolled into one, but she flaming well owes me something.'

A moment later, the woman in question appeared again. She had removed the signs of battle and only a faint flush on one cheek showed where her master had hit her.

Jackie looked at her and thought that she was the sexiest dish he had ever seen. Hansen looked at her and thought she was the most desirable woman he had ever met. Four years younger than his own thirty-two, she was beautiful, though a certain hardness spoilt her face. Born plain Edna Dodds in North Shields, she had started life as a barmaid, but her face, figure and disposition had soon brought her into the nightlife of the North. Jackie had met her in a nightclub in Doncaster and soon established her in the Rising Sun as the resident singer, a job about which she had no illusions, as sharing Jackie's bed was as much a part of the contract as murmuring throatily into a microphone.

She stalked past him now, on her way to do her second number of the evening. Laura was no great singer, but her slinky appearance and sexy delivery went down well with the virtually all-male audience.

'Ring for a taxi for me, Thor, please. About fifteen minutes.'

'I'll take you home, hinny.'

Jackie seemed set to make it up.

'Like hell you will – I want to sleep tonight. We're all going down to Middlesbrough tomorrow – remember?'

'Not till the afternoon – come on, sweetheart.'

'Fifteen minutes, Thor.'

She went out and slammed the door violently.

Jackie dropped into a chair and glowered at the Dane. 'See what I mean – if it's that bloody Geordie Armstrong, I'll kill him!'

Chapter Three

Alec Bolam threw his hat into the 'Out' tray and sank morosely into his chair, staring with distaste at the full 'In' tray. *Thank God, it can stay full until the morning*, he thought. It was Sunday and theoretically he was off duty – *as much as any detective chief inspector could ever be off duty*, he told himself sourly.

He was only in the office as an excuse to get out of the house. Last night, he'd had another flaming row with Vera. She had the sulks this morning and, rather than risk another flare-up, he had taken the car and come in to Headquarters. A couple of halves at the Corner House later on and get back by half past one for lunch – perhaps his wife might be talking to him by then. And maybe Betty, the cause of the trouble as usual, might have got up from bed.

Angrily, he jumped up and walked to the window. *What the hell is the matter with me*, he wondered?

He knew well enough, but didn't want to admit it. He'd had a lifetime of authority – as a senior police officer, as a sergeant in the Military Police … he had always been the boss, the masterful one.

Now he was up against a brick wall – a feminine, solid, unbeatable wall. His wife sided with Betty and he sensed that she was using the situation to get her own back for years of having to give in to him. Home, instead of being a place to run to, had become a good place to get out of – that was why he was hanging about Headquarters now.

He turned back to the room with a sigh. *Altogether too tidy*, he thought, staring around. The few months of occupation hadn't yet given it that patina of homeliness – the doors were still unscratched and the walls still perfectly clean. This new headquarters was all very grand and not even jerry-built. But it wasn't the same as his worn cubby hole down in the old Newcastle City HQ, which now housed 'A' Division and the Forensic Science laboratory. Since the amalgamation of the police forces into one huge organization surrounding the Tyne, everything had been turned upside-down. This in itself had done nothing to help his unsettled frame of mind.

Bolam dropped back into his chair and made an effort to feel at ease. Even his job didn't help him settle down. He had been taken off regular CID work and given odd titbits that needed special attention. Fine from the promotion point of view, he supposed, but not the same as regular work, out with the old team. At present, he was helping on a long-term fraud investigation that had dragged on for over a year and also had this nightclub racket as his special pigeon.

With the present state of affairs at home, the very mention of the word 'nightclub' was enough to make him grind his teeth and yet here he was, stuck on a job which reminded him of them all day and often half the night.

He glanced at his watch. *Twenty minutes before the pubs open.* To pass the time, he reached out and idly picked up the top paper from the overflowing tray on his desk. It was a memo from the Tyne Division, time-stamped a few hours ago. Under the new system since the Tyneside Constabulary was formed, all reports from Divisions were collected centrally and circulated daily to the people who might have an interest in what they contained.

Under this regime, Alex got a copy of any incident report, however minor, which concerned clubs or gambling premises and this one from the Tyne seemed another example of trivialities clogging the pipelines.

And yet was it?

He read the report again, more carefully.

Joe Blunt caught bashing Geordie Armstrong ... Something shifted sluggishly under the silted layers of his memory.

He tipped his chair back on two legs, his domestic worries forgotten in the light of his first love – the nicking of villains. Bolam knew that Geordie Armstrong had been spending money too freely in the last couple of months – one of his 'snouts' in the city had dropped him some information that Geordie had some kind of fiddle going. In all probability, it was connected with Geordie's job as one of Jackie Stott's croupiers.

Now Geordie gets a hammering and Bolam had little doubt that it was on Stott's orders, especially when partly confirmed by what Ernie Leadbitter said he heard as he entered the office of the *Mississippi*. They'd never be able to prove it, unless Armstrong corroborated it, which was about as likely as a reduction in Income Tax.

Bolam mused over the possibility of this being a notch in which to lever a crowbar against Jackie's empire. He could hardly see how, at present, but if he could follow up these suggestions of sharp practices in the running of the clubs, perhaps he could get a lead to something more serious. Of all the clubs on Tyneside – and there were more there than anywhere outside London – the Stott enterprises were the least desirable.

Jackie had previous convictions for violence, and so had Joe Blunt. The licences were taken out in the name of the Danish manager, who had a clean slate, as far as the British police were concerned. Alec knew that Jackie ran illegal forms of gambling on the sly, but he couldn't catch him at it. The *Mississippi*, especially, was the haunt of undesirable characters. Worse still, he knew that Stott had a nice little sideline in stolen money and the cash proceeds of other robberies. Crooks from all over the North, embarrassed by large amounts of cash, would be hard put to it if called upon to explain the source of their sudden wealth. Jackie would obligingly relieve them of the money and issue a genuine cheque – at a handsome discount – assuring them that he would swear if necessary that they had got the funds from a lucky night in his gaming rooms.

In one way or the other, Jackie Stott had become Target Number One for Alec Bolam, even apart from his own private interest in the Rising Sun Club.

The detective sighed, looked at his watch again and stuffed Leadbitter's report into his breast pocket.

Come Monday, I'll be having a word or two with Jackie.

Stott sat alone in his flat at the back of the club.

The table in front of him was littered with empty beer bottles, glasses and the stubs of small cheroots. His collar was undone and his tie pulled loose. Jackie was slightly drunk, he was jealous and he was spoiling for a fight with someone.

He had been down in Middlesbrough with Thor and Laura all the afternoon, looking at the decor of the new club. He had taken the girl down in his Mercedes, Thor Hansen using his own car. After looking the new premises over, the other two had gone off to interview a possible singer for the club; they arranged to meet him back at the Rising Sun early in the evening.

It was now well past ten o'clock and there was no sign of them. The possibility of Thor and the woman getting up to some funny business together never crossed Jackie's mind. Though generally as cunning as they come, he could be quite naive over some things. So obsessed was he with Geordie Armstrong that he refused to think of any other possibilities. Thor was above suspicion – his right hand, his prop and salvation when it came to running the clubs. Under the unobtrusive but firm guidance of the Dane, his businesses had crept from one sleazy joint three years ago to the present booming expansion. Stott had never given Thor's love life a passing thought and certainly hadn't thought of Laura being attracted by the handsome Scandinavian.

His present ill-temper was mainly due to Laura's pointed coolness over the past weeks. *Today, for instance, she hardly said a damned word all the way to Teesside,* he thought angrily. He laid the blame at Geordie's feet. *Why the hell isn't she here!* He paid her bills; he had a right to have her with him.

He gulped another beer, getting madder every moment. *She should be here, the bitch ... she's due to sing in half an hour, anyway.*

Perhaps she's persuaded Thor to take her straight home to her flat, he suddenly thought – so that she could avoid his company.

He lurched to his feet and slouched to the phone. He rang her number, but got no reply. Throwing the receiver petulantly back into its cradle, he stumped out to the fridge to get another bottle.

On the way back, he put his eye to the peephole in the wall. Everything seemed to be going all right, though there were few patrons on this particular Sunday night. He had found – or rather, Thor had advised – that it was not worth keeping the *Mississippi* open on a Sunday, so Joe Blunt, who slept aboard as caretaker, usually had the night off to do his weekly pub crawl. As he took his eye away, there was a knocking on the outer door. He cursed, it couldn't be Laura; she had her own key. The banging continued, and in a rising foul temper, he went to answer it.

Joe Blunt stood there, muffled up to his squashed nose in a shapeless overcoat and hairy scarf, a flat cap pulled down to his crumpled ears.

'What the hell do you want?'

Joe's voice penetrated the wrappings.

'Got a bit 'o news 'bout Geordie.'

Jackie stood aside to let his old retainer in.

'Bit bloody late to come bringing chit-chat, ain't it?'

Joe pulled off his coat and followed Jackie into the disordered room. He eyed the beer wistfully.

'Get a glass, then – you know where they are.'

When he was refuelled, Joe began to talk.

'Jus' now, I was in the Lambton Arms in Gallowgate. I was having a penn'orth in the lav, when I hears some fellers come in. They was a bit cut and jawing nineteen to the dozen – I could hear 'em under the door.'

'Get to the bloody point!'

But Joe was launched into his story and like a runaway steamroller, nothing could shift him from his path.

'One of 'em was saying as how he'd treat the others to another round of doubles – "flush, I am," he says – "got a lovely little racket fiddling the tables with one o' Jackie's boys." – "Oo's that then?" says another feller. "Geordie Armstrong," says the first one'

Jackie Stott was all ears now. His head stuck out and his face got redder. 'Who was it, Joe? Who the hell was it?' He was almost shouting.

Joe ground along imperturbably. 'I couldn't recognize the voice, so I gets me gear on quick and nips after 'em. Had a job, mind, but I just gets a glimpse of 'em as they got back to the Select Bar.'

'Who was it, man?' yelled Jackie, his patience gone.

'Archie Lee – that little squirt that runs a barrow on the quayside of a Sunday morning.'

Jackie was feverishly doing up the top button of his shirt and pulling up his tie. 'Archie Lee – I'll have his skin! But it's Geordie I want first. Didn't I tell you he was on the twist – didn't I?'

Joe bobbed his head owlishly, peering at Jackie who by now was pulling on his jacket.

'What's all the rush then?'

The other man was halfway to the door.

'Come on, man … where'll we find that sandy-headed bastard this time o' night? Some boozer or other; you should know which one.'

Joe trailed after him.

'He'll likely be in the Cross Inn or the Berwick Arms,' he mumbled after his boss. 'Them's his usual hang-outs, though he's been flashing it up in them smart hotels at the top end of town since he came into money.'

Stott hustled him out of the flat and slammed the door. He thundered down the stairs and got the Mercedes from his lock-up garage in the little court at the side of the club.

A moment later, they were racing through the streets, heedless of the speed limit, until a mere few hundred yards away the big white car pulled up with a jerk and Joe was hustled out at the bottom of Grainger Street to search the Cross Inn for signs of Armstrong.

'Nah, 'e ain't there,' he reported a moment later. 'Reckon he'll be in the Berwick.'

They rushed off again, this time towards the riverside. The Berwick Arms was only a short distance from the moorings of the *Mississippi*.

'Hear anything else while you was in the bog?' demanded Jackie, as they hurtled down the steep street towards the Tyne.

'Nah – only what I told you.'

'Nothing about Laura?'

'Nope, Archie Lee was only there a minute … what you going to do 'bout him?'

'I'll fix him all right. I've seen him there a few times, playing the wheel, but I didn't connect him with Geordie. They wasn't proper mates, was they?'

'Not as I know of – they couldn't have worked the fiddle if they was known to be buddies. Wonder how they did it?'

'That's what we're going to find out – amongst other

things,' snapped Jackie grimly. He went off into a string of curses which lasted almost until they pulled up outside the Berwick Arms.

'Have a look in the public bar – I'll try the snug.'

Joe began to move away, then hesitated.

'What if 'e's in there'

'Drag the bugger out. What d'yer think?' snarled Jackie impatiently. He strode off toward the left-hand door, leading to the Lounge Bar and snug.

Stopping outside the lounge door, he stared in through the old-fashioned engraved glass panel. There was a fair crowd inside, in spite of the drab surroundings.

He turned and looked into the smaller private bar. Again there was no sign of Geordie and some sixth sense stopped him going inside to make sure. He made his way out and stood fuming on the deserted pavement.

He had started to walk towards the entrance to the public bar to see what luck Joe had had, when the swing-doors opened and a body shot out as if fired from a gun.

It was Armstrong, propelled by Joe Blunt's strong right arm. He rocketed across the slippery pavement and hit the side of the Mercedes, crumpling into a heap on the ground.

Without a word, Joe and Jackie closed in on him and flung him into the front seat. Joe slipped in alongside him and Stott ran around to the driving seat. Within thirty seconds they were rolling down the quayside, headed for the gambling boat.

'What the 'ell do you think you're doing?' protested Geordie, as soon as he had got his breath back.

'It's what we're *going* to do you want to worry about,' snarled Jackie.

Geordie, who knew full well what it was all about, sank into a terrified silence.

Further along the riverside, the warehouses thinned out and various small factories, waste ground and allotments lined the river's edge where Jackie's old torpedo boat lay moored.

The white car charged up to the end of the gangway.

Almost before it stopped, both front doors opened and a petrified Armstrong was dragged out by Joe Blunt.

Struggling feebly, he was frogmarched aboard and thrust into the office.

As a preliminary, Stott gave him an open-handed slap that nearly knocked a hole in his face. This was followed up by an encore of the blasphemies that Jackie had used earlier that evening. Joe stood impassively with his back to the closed door.

'I don't know what you're gannin' on aboot,' whimpered Geordie, after the warm-up was completed. He was a dapper young man, about twenty-eight years old. *Typical ladies' man*, Jackie thought viciously, looking at his weak, pretty face.

Jackie grabbed Armstrong by the collar of his natty suit, pulled him forward until their noses were almost touching, then gave him a wicked short-arm jab in the stomach. Geordie went dead white and fainted, sagging like a bundle of rags in Jackie's hand. Impassively, he let him fall to the floor and waited for him to come around.

When he was conscious again, Stott began talking.

'How d'yer do it, Geordie – what's the fiddle with Creeper Lee?'

He kept repeating this in a dull monotone until the younger man was able to start whispering feeble denials.

Jackie grabbed him by the collar again, and he capitulated.

'Don't – I'll tell you.' Sobbing with mixed pain and fear, the story tumbled out. 'I wasn't rooking you, honest, only the mugs. Archie would come and play, early in the evening usually, when not many were about. If nobody else was on the table, I would pay him out, whatever he'd staked on … if there were others in it, I'd slip him some counters every time I paid out. Then later, he'd split fifty-

fifty with me.'

'And how d'yer reckon that wasn't fiddling me?' roared Jackie.

'That wheel has got a slight bias,' said Geordie tremulously, 'very slight, but when you spin it as often as I do, you find out. I used to fiddle the mugs when business was brisk to make up for the bit that Archie and me raked off – so it wasn't no skin off your nose, Jackie,' he ended with a whine.

'Like hell it wasn't, you little twister – that bias was still on my wheel. I should 'a been getting an even higher percentage.'

He clouted the baby-faced croupier across the face again and Geordie screamed with fright. But Jackie hadn't got down to real business by a long way.

'Been flashing the money about a bit reckless, haven't you? How much you been spending on trying to roll my Laura?'

Geordie Armstrong looked at him, speechless with surprise. He'd been resigned to a beating over the money, but this was crazy! Another crashing blow to the point of his jaw bowled him over. He felt something crack in his face, but for some reason there was no pain, or he was too dazed for it to register.

He spat some teeth as he lay on the floor, and immediately collected another kick in the chest. Mercifully, he felt numb all over, though his mind seemed clear.

'What the hell are you talking about?' he mumbled through his bloody lips.

'You know fine what I mean, damn you,' raved Jackie, as he stood over the croupier. 'My Laura, of course. You've been in her flat, haven't you! Trying your luck, eh – well, you pushed it a bit too far!'

'Dunno what – you're on – about,' gasped Geordie.

Stott kicked him viciously in the ribs a few times, then

hauled him to his feet with one great hand and rammed him back against the edge of the desk, supporting his sagging body with his fist.

'Joe, go and make sure that door is closed up on deck – I canna remember shuttin' it. This lad is going to yell some, for I'm going to half-kill him now.'

When Joe came back down a few moments later, he found that Jackie had made an understatement.

Geordie Armstrong was dead.

'He shuddnt 'a done it, Joe … he shuddnt 'a messed with my Laura!'

The two men stood looking down at the still body lying on the office floor. Both were hardened ex-fighters, with prison sentences for violence, but even they were shaken. There was all the difference between a beating-up, sadistic though it might be, and an actual killing.

'I fetched him a right hook from off the floor. He went back and hit his head on the deck. Didn't move after that. What the hell are we going to do with him, Joe?'

Joe stared at the body with his bovine expression.

'You overdone it, Jackie – you busted his neck.' He squatted down by the body and prodded it with professional interest. 'His jaw's gone as well.'

'What we going to do, I said!' snapped Jackie. He had no remorse or pity for Armstrong, only anxiety for his own skin.

'It was manslaughter – you didn't mean to croak 'im,' growled Joe, trying to be helpful.

'Ha! Do me a favour, Joe – if you think I'm going to dial nine-nine-nine and get the coppers in, you must be bloody barmy. Any fool can see he's had a duffing-up. The rozzers would die laughing – pinning a murder on me would send 'em all into hysterics.'

'What we going to do, then?'

'Didn't I jus' ask you that, you great sledge?' Stott paced up and down, slamming one fist into the other. 'Did anybody know that Geordie came aboard with us tonight? I suppose half Newcastle saw you dragging him oot that pub!'

Joe shook his bull head earnestly. 'Nah – I met him just outside the door, as he was coming out. Had a bit 'o argument with him, then flung him oot of the front door. Nobody saw us at all.'

Jackie breathed out his relief. 'Thank God for that – it's a break for us.'

Joe might well have asked why 'us' – he might be a party to grievous bodily harm but not to murder or manslaughter. But the old sparring partner was loyal. What was left of his brain, after its years of being rattled about inside his skull, contained a dog-like devotion to his protector. Without Jackie, he would have ended up in a criminal asylum – too thick to earn an honest living, he was even incapable of being a successful criminal on his own.

His mind slowly ground out the obvious solution to their dilemma. 'We'll hev te dump him in the river, then.'

The club owner nodded slowly. 'I only wish Thor could be in on this – that boy's got the best ideas on everything.'

'Least who knows about this, the better,' grunted Joe, with a flash of common sense.

Jackie went to a cabinet and took out glasses and the ever-ready bottle of whisky. 'Sure the damn door is locked?'

'Ay – we got all night, no one will disturb us. Bloody good job we're closed tonight.'

They sat and had a few stiff drinks 'to settle them' as Stott put it. He was uneducated, but had plenty of native wit. He considered the dumping of Geordie, saw the snags and as quickly thought of ways around them.

'Must make sure he stays down a long time – then he'll be so bad if he ever comes up that no one will ever recognize him.'

'What about his clobber – the coppers are clever these days,' grunted Joe.

'Take it all off and dump it separate.'

'Them copper laboratories can tell anything these days,' objected Joe – he had laboriously read an article in a recent Sunday newspaper on the subject and it had left a deep impression on his poor mind.

Jackie was impatient. 'Look, if we do it right, he ain't never going to come up – or only in little pieces.'

A sudden thought struck him. 'Who's to miss Geordie? I know he ain't married.'

Joe shook his jowls. 'He comes from down Jarrow way, but I know his family didn't bother with 'im. Since he was in the nick a few years back, his old man wouldn't have anything to do with 'im.'

'Has he got a regular woman – someone to miss him?' He refused to think of his Laura in this context.

'Don't think so – right butterfly, was Geordie. Booze and one-night stands was all he cared about.'

Jackie rubbed his hands. Things were looking pretty good. He was even beginning to feel that knocking off Armstrong was a stroke of genius, a master stroke of a big-time clubman. He forgot that a few minutes back, he was feeling sick with fear over the prospect of facing a homicide charge.

'Right, we'll strip him, shove his togs in a bag with a brick inside and dump them in't river. We'll take him down Shields way in the car and slide him in.'

Joe nodded, sharing his master's obvious satisfaction now. 'Ay, well away from here, 'case he comes up too quick.'

'He won't flaming well come up quick by the time I've finished with him.' Confidence was rapidly changing into bravado. 'But best keep well clear of here, no sense in dirtying our own doorstep.'

They finished their drinks, and set about stripping

Geordie's body.

Then Joe picked up Armstrong's narrow-lapelled jacket and dipped a hand into the pockets. He tossed some small change, keys and a wallet on to the desk. 'What we going to do with these?'

Jackie went through the wallet and transferred some twenty pound notes to his own pocket. 'Reckon he owes me a lot more than that,' he grunted. He pawed through the papers in the wallet to make sure there were no love letters from Laura lurking there, then slung it down on to the pile of clothing. 'Dump it with the togs – don't want nothing to be traced from him.'

Joe helped himself to the loose change, then stuffed all the clothing into a plastic bag that he found in the cleaner's cupboard. 'I got nothin' to weight it with,' he mumbled.

'Let's get the body into the back of the Merc. Then you can find some junk on the quayside,' commanded Stott.

They wrapped the body in a curtain unhooked from over the toilet door and carried it upstairs, the weight being nothing to the two powerful men.

'Leave him here inside the door – I'll back the car up.'

Jackie reversed the white Mercedes so that the boot was almost touching the end of the gangway. Then he came back, watched and listened for a moment, but nothing moved in the cold mist of the riverside. They hustled the bundle out and dropped it into the big boot.

Jackie slammed the lid and waited in the car, while Joe trudged off along the quayside, looking in the gloom for a brick. A few yards away, he came across a heap of unidentifiable metal junk, amongst it a short length of angle-iron weighing several pounds. Joe slid it into the bag and tied the neck in a rough knot. Walking to the wharfside, he slid it over, hearing a satisfying splash as it hit the water.

He hurried back to the car and it slithered off in a burst of acceleration towards Shields Road.

As soon as the noise of its exhaust had faded, a tall figure stepped out of the gritty mist at the side of an old warehouse. On crepe-soled feet, he padded to the water's edge just where Joe had thrown his bundle. Staring down into the black water, he saw with satisfaction that the ebbing tide had already exposed a little rim of filthy mud and stones immediately below him.

He looked around the wharf to make sure that he could fix the spot exactly when the tide was right down, then walked off into the mist.

Chapter Four

Jackie Stott was a pretty tough nut, but even *his* stomach gave a nasty lurch when, first thing next morning, he was visited by a detective chief inspector.

A moment later, he kicked himself for his stupidity, as he knew very well that Alec Bolam was concerned only with clubs and gaming, not murder.

When Bolam called, Jackie was sitting at a table in the empty main room of the Rising Sun.

Every Monday, there was a ritual meeting, when Thor Hansen went through the previous week's business. As Hansen rattled off strings of figures, Jackie leaned back in his chair, a mini cigar clamped between his lips. His ears were deaf to business matters. His mind was on the body that now lay twenty feet down in the mud of the Tyne. He was not particularly uneasy about it – he reckoned that there was no reason why it shouldn't stay down there for years. There was no one to go clamouring to the police about Geordie's disappearance and it might be months before his family got curious as to his whereabouts. And as far as Jackie was concerned, Geordie Armstrong had left his job and gone to London to seek his fortune!

While he was daydreaming against the background of Hansen's financial droning, Bolam's raincoated figure appeared silently inside the glass doors. He was almost at the table before Stott noticed him and his first words were tailor-made to give the club owner the maximum shock.

'What you been doing to Geordie Armstrong, then, Jackie?'

While Stott sat frozen to his seat with shock, the detective pulled out another chair and plumped down uninvited. Jackie stared at him in fascination, his mind momentarily seized up.

The Danish manager stopped his recital and looked from one to the other with his usual impassive expression fixed in place.

Jackie rapidly took a grip on himself.

'What the hell d'yer mean?'

In spite of his efforts, his voice sounded like an old hacksaw.

Alec Bolam ran a hand over his jet black hair. 'Our river lads tell me you had a bit of trouble on Saturday night. I hope we're not going to have any strong-arm routines on any of your premises.'

You bleeding liar, thought Jackie, *you'd like nothing better*. But he was relieved; this was only a check-up on that damn fool Joe.

'Divvent worry yourself about that, Inspector. Our poor old Joe is getting weaker in the pan than ever. You know how he is!'

Bolam allowed himself a weak, official smile.

'I know that Sergeant Leadbitter heard you tell Joe that you wanted Armstrong duffed up a bit.'

Stott rasped his chair back and planted his hands aggressively on the table. 'He heard bloody wrong, then!'

'The sergeant had a witness – his constable,' retorted Bolam.

'Then they're both bloody liars.'

'Come off it, Jackie! Ernie Leadbitter should have pulled Joe in on the strength of that. Breach of the peace, disorderly conduct on licensed premises … what had Geordie been up to?'

Jackie had to think fast. Should he stick to a flat denial or spin some yarn to satisfy Bolam? Knowing the chief inspector, he hesitated to try the first.

'All right, then, it was a storm in a flaming teacup.' He

put on a falsely contrite expression and tried to pass the thing off. 'Joe is as jealous as hell of Geordie – divvent ask me why. He saw Armstrong slipping a coupla gaming tokens in his pocket and came and told me. Naturally I don't want any sharp practices like that in my place,' he went on righteously, 'so I had it out with Geordie.'

Bolam sat with a sardonic grin on his face, but he kept silent.

'He got right nasty, so I told him to shove off and never come back – rather have a croupier short than a crooked one. He turned violent and took a poke at me, so I told Joe to throw him out … the bit about a duffing-up was a bit hasty, I admit, but he *had* taken a swing at me!'

He finished on a note of injured penitence which rang about as true as a ninepenny wineglass in Bolam's ears.

'You're breaking my heart, Jackie,' he said sarcastically, 'What's Geordie got to say about all this'

Jackie had another nasty feeling in the pit of his stomach.

'Dunno – better ask him, if you can find him. I gave him the push Sat'dy night, naturally. Haven't seen him since – don't want to, neither!'

He lolled back with an air of finality.

Alec Bolam opened the buttons of his gabardine, as if settling down for a long talk. 'Mind if I look around?' he said.

'Help yoursel',' replied Jackie in a surly voice.

Bolam got up and walked around. He was not looking for anything particular, only making his presence felt. He had another private reason, too. Standing in front of the band platform, he stared at the mute set of drums, his face as black as thunder. In a moment, he turned and the expression had gone.

He moved towards the door, buttoning up his coat.

'I'll be having a word with Geordie, to get his version. Where's he live?'

Jackie cursed under his breath. This was the very thing he had wanted to avoid – *blast Joe Blunt and his thickheaded stupidity.*

'No idea – never asked him,' he said with a flippancy he didn't feel.

Bolam's eyebrows went up. 'No address? He's your employee. Didn't you pay National Health, PAYE – all the rest of it?'

Jackie muttered some choice blasphemies under his breath as he turned to Thor Hansen.

'I suppose you'll have it somewhere?'

Thor nodded and left his chair. 'In the office – I'll get it for you, Mr Bolam.' He went to the small partitioned office next to Herbert Lumley's cubicle.

While the Dane was away, Alec asked Stott about him. 'Got no secrets from him, eh? He seems the mainstay of this place. I hope none of your crooked ways rub off on him.'

Jackie flushed. 'Watch it, copper. I got convictions, I know, but I paid for them with plenty of bird, so now it's quits. Hansen's straight, so am I. So screw that sort of talk!'

Bolam was unperturbed. 'One of these days, you're going to give one of your famous cheques for some money that's got numbered notes … then we'll have you inside so fast that you'll leave your boots behind.'

Bolam was bluffing and Stott knew it.

'Tell that to your poor ol' granny, mate! I never done such a thing in me life, but even if I had, you could never make a receiving charge stick. What gets passed across my gaming tables is up to the mugs – I mean, *patrons*. I got no control over it, hot money or not!'

Hansen came back with a slip of paper, so stopping the development of an argument. Jackie snatched it and read the address.

'Somewhere in the West End – unless he's moved.

They never stay long in one place, these lads.'

Alec Bolam took the paper with a murmur of thanks.

'Will you be off to see him now?' asked Jackie with feigned casualness. ''Cos I reckon you'll have a wasted journey. He'll be in the Smoke by now. Plenty of jobs for a card-sharper there, especially as I'm going to blackball him in every club in the North.'

Bolam shrugged.

'I'll send one of my boys to check on him sometime – there's always the hope that they can persuade him to make a charge against you and Joe for assault!'

With this parting shot, he strode out of the club.

'Bastard!' said Jackie with feeling, as soon as the doors had swung behind the detective.

'What's this about Geordie getting the sack?' asked Thor, his blue eyes settling steadily on Stott's perspiring face. 'You told me on Saturday that you only *felt* like firing him.'

Jackie cursed under his breath. The meshwork of lies was already starting to trip him up. The only course was to tell half the truth.

'I was going to tell you – you won't be seeing him around again. I gave him the push last night.'

'What happened?' Hansen had a shrewd idea already of the circumstances, but wanted to see how Stott would wriggle out of it.

'Joe heard that Geordie and a layabout called Archie Lee had been running a swindle on us. I told you I suspected it, didn't I?' He ran a finger around the sweaty neckband of his collar. 'Look, for Gawd's sake keep this to yourself, or we'll have the pollis down on us again like a ton of bricks ... Joe and I ran Armstrong to earth in the Cross Inn last night. We twisted his arm a bit and I whispers in his ear that if he's anywhere north of the Humber by midday today, I'll set Joe on him properly. And that's it – he's taken a powder.'

41

Thor looked inscrutably at his employer.

'You didn't rough him up?'

Jackie looked offended.

'In the middle of Grainger Street? Do me a favour!'

Hansen decided not to pursue the matter any more, for his own reasons. He tried to change the subject back to the unfinished club business but, at this, Jackie suddenly stood up.

'Skip the rest of the accounts for this week – I'm not in the mood. That damn copper always sours me.'

He hurried down to the garage to get out the Mercedes. Driving to the *Mississippi*, he found his henchman vacuum cleaning the office floor.

'None of that blood got on the carpet, thank Gawd,' grunted Joe. 'I've rubbed down all the furniture and doorknobs.'

Jackie nodded impatiently, not bothering to tell him that he'd been wasting his time. 'Here's a couple of fivers – get down to London on the first train. I want you to send a telegram.'

By lunchtime, Bolam had managed to make a sizeable dent in the contents of his 'In' tray. To stretch his legs, he walked down to Burgoyne's in Newgate Street for a pint and a hot pie, then came back to continue 'hammering the bumf', as he called it.

Five minutes after starting, he didn't know whether to be glad or sorry for an interruption. The door opened without ceremony and a cheerful figure barged in.

'He's skipped all right, but his clothes are still there.'

Tall and tough, like most Newcastle policemen, Jimmy Grainger seemed to half-fill the room.

Alec grunted as he looked up at his detective sergeant. 'Then Jackie must have put the fear of God into him, if he scarpered without his gear. He was a snappy dresser, like all that mob at Jackie Stott's dive.'

Again the bitterness welled up. Grainger recognized it and tactfully eased the subject away.

'Want me to follow it up – ask the Met to trace him?'

Alec shook his head. 'Not worth the trouble. We've only got Stott's word that he's gone to London … and we know what *his* word is worth. Geordie's probably lurking in some Merseyside cellar club by now.'

Jimmy ran a hand through his wiry hair … he was another blond, who could have stepped straight off the streets of Oslo or Stockholm. 'You want me to pack in this Armstrong thing, then. I got plenty else to do, I'll tell you.'

Bolam nodded at him over the next bit of 'bumf'. Grainger was only on part-time assignment to him. As well as being involved in the gaming job, the sergeant dabbled in Aliens, Firearms, and Drugs.

'Jack of all bloody trades, that's me!' he said cheerfully, hauling himself to his full six feet one.

'And master of none! If you're so busy, why are you loafing round here?'

Grainger raised his hands in mock defence.

'OK, OK, I'm going. Think I'll spend the afternoon in the pictures, to make sure there's no unregistered aliens in the audience.'

As he reached the door, Alec swung round in his swivel chair. 'What did Geordie's landlord say about him leaving his belongings?'

'Didn't seem too surprised. Sounded as if he hoped he'd never come back for 'em.'

'The owner hadn't had word from him, then?'

'No – it's only a day since Jackie gave him the sack, mind. Apparently, Geordie had already given notice to quit, but he had a couple of weeks to work out his monthly rent.'

'You didn't go in to see his room?'

'No, didn't think you were that interested … want me to go back?'

Alec shrugged. 'No hurry … when you think of it, just to tie up the loose ends.'

The detective sergeant nodded and left, leaving Bolam to reach out with a sigh for the next piece of paper.

On the following evening, Jackie Stott sat behind a glass of whisky at one of the back tables in the big club room of the Rising Sun.

For a Tuesday, the crowd was very good, over half the tables being filled by ten thirty. Laura was in the middle of her first number. The audience were quiet and attentive, which was just as well, as Jackie would personally have dealt with anyone who dared create a rumpus whilst his bird was singing.

Their attentiveness was not so much because of her voice, but because of her figure. None of the men, except the few in a sentimentally drunken state, took much notice of the ballad she was whispering secretively into the hand-mike. But they all stared goggle-eyed at her legs. Laura wore a minidress of some glittery material which stopped abruptly at upper thigh level. With that outfit on, she could have been reciting Pythagoras' Theorem set to music for all the crowd cared.

Jackie sat contentedly, a glass in one hand and a thin cheroot in the other. Apart from the Geordie incident, and Laura's coolness, things seemed to be going very well.

That was a nasty moment when Bolam came snooping around, he thought, but he had outsmarted the coppers again. A warm glow of self-congratulation spread through his soul and he downed the rest of his drink in celebration. A finger crooked in the direction of the bar brought the barmaid at a gallop. She gave him another whisky and a big smile. Freda was a busty brunette, whom Jackie had in mind as a second string if anything happened to Laura – not that he wanted anything to happen to her, so long as she dropped this iceberg routine.

As his crooning mistress continued to wriggle her hips at the 'mugs' while seemingly doing her best to swallow the microphone, Jackie began painting rosy pictures of the Stott nightclub empire. Thanks to Thor Hansen, the two in Newcastle were prospering and this one in Middlesbrough could hardly fail to be another success. Then …

He came back to earth as Laura finished and made her way over to his table, giving false smiles in reply to the hopeful leers of the men as she threaded between them.

'Christ, gimme a gin and tonic! The air in here is like sewer gas!' she said.

Jackie snapped his fingers and Freda came over again, noticeably slower this time and without the welcoming smile, when she saw Laura sitting with Jackie.

The drink arrived and with it came Thor Hansen, who had been watching the play upstairs.

'Fair crowd tonight, Thor,' observed Jackie expansively.

'Lecherous lot of swine!' cut in Laura. 'Can feel them undressing you with their eyes.'

Stott grinned. 'Your bread and butter, pet – perhaps you ought to do the strip instead of Rita!'

The woman gave him a look that would have loosened the teeth of anyone less tough than Jackie. 'Don't know why the hell I do it – I'm not appreciated round here, that's the trouble.'

'*I* appreciate you, pet.' Jackie stretched out a hand and put it on her bare back. The dress, though high in front, dipped to the waist behind.

She twitched angrily to shake him off. 'Lay off, will you, Jackie,' she hissed. 'In front of all these damn goons!'

His lips tightened and his cheerful mood began to fade. The Dane sensed the bad atmosphere between the two and stepped in with his usual tact to change the subject. 'Looks as if we're going to have a day free from the police.'

Jackie scowled. 'That Bolam is getting a pest. What the

hell does he think he's going to gain by creeping in here all the time?'

'The other clubs get him, too – especially Eddie Freeman's – so we're not being singled out exclusively.'

Jackie shook his big head angrily. 'He comes here a damn sight more than Eddie's and, God knows, Freeman is up to his neck in every racket in the book. So why does he hang around here?'

'If you don't know that, you're even dafter than I thought,' snapped Laura, with icicles in her voice, and jerked her head across the room to a table near the band rostrum. 'Who d'you think she is, then?'

Jackie stared at the place Laura had pointed out. At the table, a small one tucked against the wall, a dark girl of about twenty sat alone. This in itself was nothing unusual in Jackie's place, but the girls *he* knew were always there on business. This one was a world apart from them. She was quite good-looking, but by no means outstanding. The main point he noticed was that she gazed fixedly at the four-man music group on the stage. With chin resting on a hand, her eyes never left them.

'What you trying to say, Laura?' he snapped irritably.

'You'll see when the boys finish murdering that tune,' she retorted. The discordant wailing of an electric guitar, double bass, and electronic organ died with a final thump of drums and cymbal.

The Rising Sun audience were not the type to bother with applause for mere musicians and almost before the echoes had faded, the performers were on their way to the bar. All except one, the guitarist. He made his way across to the corner table where he kissed the dark girl, then sat down holding her hand across the Formica top.

'See!' exclaimed Laura, triumphantly.

Jackie looked at her, baffled. 'So what?'

The singer looked at him pityingly. 'That's Bolam's daughter,' she said.

Jackie Stott's pale eyes opened wider. A low whistle escaped him. 'Bolam's girl with Freddie Robson! Well, what d'yer know! I never thought he had it in him.'

'Freddie – why not?' snapped Laura.

'Because if Freddie's not a poof, I'm a monkey's uncle!'

Laura managed to resist the obvious retort to this, but snapped at him again. 'That's all an act, you idiot. He's all there, is Freddie. That girl's been coming in for a month or more now. She's mad keen on Freddie – not on his guitar playing, either!'

Jackie grinned and rubbed his hands. 'I don't know how, but this looks like a stick to beat Bolam with ... any ideas, Thor?'

The tall Dane kept his impassive look firmly in place.

'Not really – I can't see any need to beat the police at present. Apart from taking up a few minutes of our time, they haven't bothered us ... we've nothing to hide, have we?'

The last words carried a subtle sarcasm, but they were lost on Jackie's insensitive ears.

A sudden thought struck him. 'She's not a minor, is she? ... for God's sake don't let Daddy find some excuse to fix us with his own daughter.' He looked a little wild-eyed for a moment. 'Hey, perhaps he's planted her here for that – or some other bloody mischief.'

Laura looked at him as if he had just crawled from under a stone. 'Relax. Your imagination is like some fifth-rate movie ... she's over twenty-one, as it happens – a month or more past.'

Jackie scowled again. 'How come you seem so well in with Bolam's family affairs? You think she's a rival for you over Freddie now?'

Laura almost spat in his face. 'If you must know, Freddie told me that he met the Bolam girl at her twenty-first birthday party. Probably the one and only time he'll ever set foot in her old man's house!'

Stott made no reply, but stood up and brushed the cigar ash from the front of his well-filled suit.

'Tell Freddie I want to see him in the office, Thor.'

He went out to the small room in the foyer and in a few moments, Freddie Robson came in rather nervously.

He was a pretty, fair-haired lad, slimly built and somewhat girlish-looking, but by no means deserved Jackie's label of 'queer'. Twenty-six, single, and an indifferent musician, he was good enough for the quartet that provided the noise at the Rising Sun.

'Sit down, Freddie. Let's have a few words.'

Jackie was full of false heartiness.

Freddie groped for a chair and promptly knocked it over. He picked it up and nervously sat down facing the boss.

'Have a fag?' Jackie smoked small cigars, but always carried cigarettes to hand out.

Freddie extended a shaking hand and, in trying to get hold of one, knocked the whole packet on to the desk.

'Take it easy, chum, I'm not going to bleeding eat you,' snapped Stott. 'I want to know about your girlfriend.'

'Betty?' Freddie asked, in surprise.

Jackie nodded. 'You know she's a top copper's kid?'

The guitarist nodded spasmodically. 'Yeah – I bin to their house once.'

'First and last time, eh?'

'Yus … her old man is all set to skin me alive if he can find an excuse. Hates me like poison.'

'Why's that then?' asked Stott.

Freddie Robson shrugged his thin shoulders. 'Dunno, really. Because I ain't a copper, because I ain't his type …'

'And because you work for me in this club!' completed Jackie.

Freddie nodded. 'That's about it, Mr Stott. He's as mad

48

as hell. Just about busted up their home life, Betty says.'

Freddie doesn't seem too broken up about the prospect, thought Jackie. 'Where do you fit into this, lad – you go for her?'

Freddie shrugged again. 'She's a good kid.'

'What's that mean – you want to marry her or something?'

'Hell no, I'm not the marrying kind. Lay 'em and leave 'em, that's me.'

Jackie Stott erupted into a great burst of laughter and slapped Freddie on the shoulder, almost breaking the delicate boy's arm. 'Great, man … and have you?'

'Have I what?'

'Laid her, you nit!'

Freddie shook his head. 'No … she's different from most. Part of the attraction. She's High School and got a strong daddy – all that crap. She wants to, but won't give in easy.' He looked reflectively at his shaking fingernails. 'I'm in no hurry – once I make it, it'll be "cheerio" … know what I mean?'

Jackie beamed and gave Freddie a great man-of-the-world nod. 'Look here, Freddie. Her old man is on my back over this club business. I want to get at him, so you pull out all the stops with his kid, right? Get her really on the boil, but don't actually do it until I say the word … *if* I say it.'

Freddie looked at his boss in surprise. 'What's the idea … you want me to commit hara-kiri with her old man! I gotta box clever as it is or he'll murder me.'

Jackie raised his hand. 'Leave it to Uncle Jackie, Freddie! Look, you can even suggest marrying her, if it helps … yeah, that's a good tack, that. Get her lined up for the ring and registrar.'

The guitarist goggled at him.

'Marry her! Gawd, have a heart!'

Jackie waved his hand. 'Don't worry, it'll never come

off. I just want to be able to put the squeeze on her old man. You just lay on the bloody charm, Freddie. I'll make it worth your while, never fear.'

Freddie saw a glimmer of light and nodded dubiously. 'Hope you will, Mr Stott. Getting foul of Alec Bolam is like sitting on a flaming landmine. I'm half scared to even pass a copper in the street these days, for fear he'll have me in the nick … 'specially over the little sideline I'm running.'

He stopped speaking suddenly, afraid that he might have said too much.

Jackie just grinned. 'That's your business, laddie … though if I were you, I'd stick to Newcastle Brown Ale and women, and leave the other stuff alone.'

He jerked his head in dismissal and Freddie weaved his way out. Jackie wondered idly whether his guitar playing would be any better for a few puffs of a reefer now and then, instead of the pep pills.

Chapter Five

Looking back on the whole affair, Alec Bolam would have agreed that the next day of that week – the Wednesday – as when everything really began to get on the boil. At the time, however, the varied events of the day were just unconnected happenings.

Late in the afternoon, Bolam went along to see his chief superintendent on some routine matter. When this was dealt with, he stayed for a smoke and a chat. The head of Tyneside CID was a craggy Scotsman named MacDonald.

'How's the battle going then, Alec?' he asked.

'Very slow, sir. I don't know whether the rogues are getting more cunning or more honest, but there's been hardly a thing around the clubs these past few weeks. Thought I had something to hang on Eddie Freeman, but I doubt if it'll stick.'

'What's that'

'Oh, the old chestnut about harbouring toms in his place. We know fine that the girls hang about there, but he says if they pay their membership fees, he can't stop them – and who they sleep with after the club shuts is none of his business.'

MacDonald nodded. 'He'll say naught about the backhander he gets from them for using his place for the old come-on … it's a damned hard charge to survive a good defence lawyer – and we're cursed with enough of those in this city, God knows!'

'Anything else?' he asked after a moment.

'A bit of a punch-up on Jackie Stott's boat, that's all.
The Scotsman's curly grey eyebrows went up a trifle. He

wanted to hear all the details. 'And didn't this Armstrong make a charge?' he asked at the end.

Bolam turned up his palms. 'Dunno – no one's seen him since. I sent Grainger around to his digs, but he's gone. The sergeant tried again today, just for the record, but his landlord had had a telegram from London saying that he wasn't coming back. Wanted his stuff packed up, ready for forwarding. Jackie Stott must have scared the daylights out of him.'

'Was he on the fiddle'

'Probably – one less villain in the town.'

MacDonald sighed. 'Always another to take his place.'

The conversation drifted on to other things, just as the curtain rose on another scene in the drama, at a spot eight miles away, where a Tyne Division launch was leaving the River Headquarters at South Shields. It was a routine patrol, on the other beat from Ernie Leadbitter's section.

This boat had the wider, busier part of the river, from the shipyards at Wallsend and Jarrow down to the great piers which jutted out pugnaciously into the grey North Sea.

The launch, *F for Fox* this time, growled away from the Mill Dam jetty and headed down river towards the sea. Mike Milburn was the sergeant in charge, a younger man than Leadbitter, but with plenty of experience on the river and, before that, in the Navy.

He and his constable had done the up-river section of their beat on the first part of the shift and were now setting off for a leisurely circuit of the seaward end before it got dark. The fine December morning had given way to a mist with a threat of snow. At three-thirty, visibility was already poor. They slid between a pair of colliers waiting at the buoys and headed along the south bank of the river.

'Quite lively these past few days, sarge.'

This driver was a talker, unlike Horace. He was talking about ships, not crime, nodding at the clutter of vessels in the lower reaches of the river.

Milburn looked around, his sailor's eyes identifying all the different craft. 'Marvellous how quickly it can change – might come out in the morning and see damn all here!'

The views slowly altered as they moved downstream as far as the hailing station opposite the pilot jetty. There was nothing beyond except the great open triangle of water between the granite piers. The constable swung the police launch around and by the time they got up to Smith's Dock again, the light had almost gone.

As usual, their thoughts turned to the imminent 'cuppa' back in the station office, but when they were level with a rusty old dredger, Milburn looked curiously through the side window at the ugly craft.

'What the hell they doing on the bucket-dredger – having a strike or summat?'

More from the reflected lights of the docks and ships than from the sky, he could see a group of figures clustered on the bow of the clumsy vessel. Then there was a thin, bleating wail and a jet of steam from her funnel.

'She's blowing her flipping hooter!' exclaimed the constable from the driving seat. He sounded incredulous. 'I never heard that in seven year on t' river. Didn't even know she had a one!'

The sergeant slid back the Perspex side window and stuck his head out for a better look. 'I think they're waving at us – there's the siren again. Take her over there, something's going on.'

The constable racked his wheel around and they swerved across towards the dredger which was moored both to the dockside and to buoys out in the river. By winching itself back and forth between these, it moved slowly sideways while scooping the mud from outside the dry dock gates.

As they cruised up to it, Milburn could see that the

crew were waving wildly at them. The great wheel at the top of the pithead device had stopped and the endless chain of huge buckets had ground to a halt.

When they came alongside, Milburn clambered onto the launch's gunwale and threw a rope to a ready hand on the dredger.

'What's all the panic – you been torpedoed?'

'We was just going to send a boat ashore to ring up the station – then we saw you coming up river … we just raised a body.'

The sergeant sighed. Their Division recovered a dead body from the river at least once a fortnight, so another would be no novelty. 'Let's have a look at it, then.'

He jumped aboard and marched forward along the rusty deck.

Though it was virtually dark, the bow of the dredger was well-lit, thanks to a battery of lamps hanging overhead. The rest of the crew were clustered around the deep slot in the centre of the vessel, where the chain of buckets vanished into the black water.

'Hasn't got a bloody stitch on, sarge.'

The captain of the dredger came up to Milburn and led him across the tangle of chains and cables to the side of the dredging well. He pointed at the third bucket from the bottom, which was about level with the deck.

From the lip of the great steel scoop, a curious white object stuck out. It took Milburn several seconds to realize that it was the bare backside of a human body. The head and feet were doubled up inside the bucket, which was big enough to hold three men.

Bewick, his constable, came stumping along the deck behind him, having secured the police launch to the side of the dredger.

'Another drowner – stuck in a bucket this time,' report Milburn.

'Makes a change – being in t' scoop, I mean,' observed

Bewick phlegmatically. 'How do we get him oot?'

Eventually, the dredger boss decided to hoist the bucket boom from the water. The great scoops travelled in an endless belt around a long arm, which was pivoted at the top, twenty feet above the deck. The boom was winched up and as the buckets became more and more horizontal, mud and water gushed from them.

'For God's sake, don't tip him out!' warned Milburn in alarm, as the buttocks gave a sudden lurch.

The winch stopped wheezing and the two policemen scrambled on to the boom, slipping on the treacherous coating of black Tyne mud. One on each side of the bucket, they clung to its lip and peered in. There was still a lot of water and sludge inside and no head nor feet could be seen.

'Pretty fresh – though in this weather, he might as well be in a fridge.'

Milburn's implied decision about the gender of the remains was confirmed by the view they had of the body.

'Right, let's be having him,' muttered Bewick.

'Want a sling on him?' called the dredger man.

In a moment, a coir rope was slung over some structure above and dangled down into the bucket. The policemen then ran a clove hitch around the hips of the corpse.

'Haul away!' called Milburn, stepping back off the bucket boom to avoid the shower of filth that would drip off the body as it rose.

With an obscene squelch, it came away from its inelegant sepulchre as two crewmen heaved on the bight of the rope. The waist jackknifed, and the extremities appeared, deformed and bulbous in a glutinous cocoon of mud.

'Turn a hose on it?' offered the helpful captain.

Milburn, trained to preserve any evidence of unusual events, hesitated a moment. Then he shrugged – this was just another 'drowner' that had already been swirling around in the river for goodness knows how many days. Habit died hard, but he raised a hand to agree.

'Leave it till we get it on the deck – a bit more mud on your plates won't hurt. You're not the flaming *Queen Elizabeth*.'

A few seconds later, he blessed his caution. As the body swung gently overhead, he put up a hand to pull it to one side as the men lowered away. Instead of meeting slithery wet skin, his fingers closed over twisted metal.

Two minutes later he was crouched over the radio in the police boat, his voice brittle with excitement as he called up Control Room.

'*F for Fox* to Tynepol Control … listen, Charlie, get those CID characters on to a boat, pronto! Over to the dredger lying off Smith's Docks. Tell 'em to step on it … we've just raised a body – stark naked and with the arms and legs tied together with wire!'

An hour later, Bucket-Dredger No. 7 was crawling with people.

There were three police boats tied alongside, as well as the *Vidette*, the big blue launch of the harbourmaster, who was responsible for the dredger's activities.

The River Division had a CID branch of their own, but for anything as important as a possible murder, the Headquarters CID in Newcastle took over. The third launch, just arrived, brought many of these, including Chief Superintendent MacDonald, the photography and fingerprints team, together with Dr Ellison, the Home Office pathologist and a scientist from the laboratory. This group had travelled by road to North Shields and made the last short lap by water.

'Uncle Mac' was soon firmly in charge. 'Let the dogs see the rabbit, boys … Harbourmaster, could you shift all your fellows clear, please. Let's have a nice clear area around the patient. Give him some air, now.'

This macabre wit raised a few sniggers, but it also cleared the decks.

'Right, let's have some pictures for a start!'

The next few moments were spent in curses from the photographers as they tried to set up their tripods on the slimy deck. Eventually, the night was torn by electronic flashes which competed with the welding glares on nearby tankers.

MacDonald talked with Milburn and Bewick, then with some of the dredger men, while the cameras rolled. The next two actors on the scene stood quietly smoking in the background, years of practice at waiting having told them that it was useless to bustle around and get in other people's way.

Their turn eventually came.

'Right, Doc and Mr Burke – it's all yours,' rumbled the old Scot. 'Fight it out between you, which wants first pick at the chicken.'

The forensic pathologist and the man from the laboratory decided to perform a duet this time. They crouched one on each side of the slimy mess on the deck. More lights had been rigged up and they had almost too good a view of the mud-encrusted remains. The body had not been touched since Milburn had had it lowered to the steel plating. The top and bottom ends were still thickly enshrouded in black ooze.

The two boffins murmured between themselves, then the pathologist, a rotund little man with an angry, bright red face, spoke to the detective chief superintendent.

'We'll have to clean him off somehow. As he's been in the river and bashed about by the dredger buckets, anything that was going to be lost has already gone, so we can use a gentle hosing-down.'

A small hosepipe was produced and a stream of water helped the two scientists to delicately sluice the Tyne mud from the body. Squatting there, silhouetted in the harsh glare of the lamps, they looked to Milburn and Bewick like two vultures, or vampires in some horror film.

The man from the laboratory was a pale, thin man in his thirties, suffering from the unfortunate name of Gasgoine Burke. He had thick horn-rimmed spectacles and wild, straggly hair.

He spoke now in a surprisingly firm, deep voice. 'Galvanized fencing wire – three turns on the ankles, two on the wrists.'

MacDonald was standing close by, looking on intently.

'Bound to be murder, then?'

Ellison hopped to his feet. 'No, no, no ... not necessarily. I've seen a couple of suicides who tied their feet together, to stop themselves swimming.'

'And the wrists?' The arty young man's voice was deep with sarcasm.

The pathologist throttled back a notch. 'Well, I've never seen it myself – but it has been described.'

'With fence wire as stiff as this?' demanded Burke.

He and the doctor were old antagonists.

Ellison snorted, but the scientist persisted.

'Come on – and do they strip themselves naked first?'

He bent down again to join the doctor, their differences forgotten in the interest of the moment. Together they cautiously lifted the body sideways and looked at the back. The hose was worked gently about until most of the mud was off.

'No sign of bullet or stab wounds,' commented Gasgoine.

'Nor strangulation – though part of the neck has been ripped off by the bucket,' contributed Ellison. He let the corpse flop back on to the plating. 'In fact, nothing very obvious, except these bruises.'

He pointed to mottled marks on the sides of the chest and loins.

After a few more minutes of poking about, with silent policemen watching them, the two Home Office men got to their feet.

'No more we can do here – mortuary's the next thing,' said Ellison.

This sparked off another argument.

'The hospital won't have it – it's covered in stinking mud and although it's all right now, it'll be pretty "ripe" in a day or two,' offered the doctor.

MacDonald shrugged. 'Have to go to the public mortuary then … none of 'em have got fridges, so we may as well take it up to Newcastle.'

The remains were carefully wrapped in a canvas stretcher with a polythene lining and taken aboard one of the launches for the journey up to the city.

Milburn and Bewick watched it leave.

'Like a bloody state funeral!' the sergeant said scathingly. 'C'mon, let's get across for that cuppa.'

While the morbid cavalcade was advancing up the Tyne, Alec Bolam was just arriving home, oblivious of the murder. He was not to be involved for at least another day, as his present duties were far removed from murder investigations.

He swung the car into the driveway of his semidetached villa and left it there, as he was going round the clubs later on. He stuck his key in the front door, wondering with a sigh what sort of reception awaited him on the other side.

His wife was standing at the other end of the hall, at the door of the kitchenette.

'Why haven't you put the car away?' she snapped.

No word of welcome, he thought, resisting the urge to open the door again and step back into the peace of the street outside. 'Hello, pet – I've got to go out again later on.' He was determined not to start anything – let her do it, then he could salve his conscience by telling himself it was all her fault. 'Everything all right?' he added.

This apparently merited no reply. Vera Bolam vanished into the kitchen. He hung up his coat and hat and wandered morosely into the lounge. It was a modern house, with one long room stretching from front to back, the kitchen and hall being at the side.

His wife's head jerked into the serving hatch.

'You're early. You'll have to wait on Betty for your tea.'

The grim face snapped back out of sight. Alec sank into an easy chair alongside the glowing fire. He picked up the *Evening Chronicle* and shook it open. Though his eyes followed the lines of print, his mind was hardly registering. For the thousandth time, he wondered why marriage should be such a hell of a thing after starting with such promise.

True, this business with Betty and that damned poof had brought things to a head but, even before that, they'd had a good many cool years. Vera was still an attractive woman at forty-two, a year younger than himself. She came in now and set the table, without giving him a glance. Neither said anything.

His wife had an aura of tenseness and Alec held his tongue. He knew that whatever he said, even if it was about the weather, would light the fuse of some new outburst. To occupy himself, he picked up the poker and made a vicious attack on the fire.

'Trying to ruin it? It's been all right all day and now you come and make a mess of it – look at the dust you're raising!'

The words snicked out like the flashing of a rapier, all the more effective because he knew she was right – he was wrecking a perfectly good fire.

Flinging the poker down, he jumped to his feet. 'OK, OK, but for God's sake, can't you say something pleasant – just for once?'

She sneered at him. 'I might – if *you* did! You use this place like a lodging-house. In and out at all times, face like a fiddle …'

The usual row began, but was interrupted by the sound of another key in the front door. They both stopped. 'No fighting in front of the child' had been the rule for so many years that they still kept the habit, though the 'child' was now a grown woman.

Vera Bolam hurried out to meet her daughter and the murmur of female voices was abruptly cut off by the slamming of the hatch.

Alec breathed heavily and snapped on the television in reprisal. The six o'clock news was just finishing and the local *Look North* news magazine came on the screen. '… just reported that members of Tyneside Criminal Investigation Department were called to a dredger at North Shields late this afternoon when a body was recovered from the River Tyne. Apart from the fact that foul play could not be ruled out, a police spokesman would make no comment, but a Press release is expected later this evening.'

Alec raised his eyebrows at the little screen. To his experienced ears, this phraseology suggested that 'something was up'. He had left Headquarters fairly early and had heard nothing about any flap. It was none of his business, but anything that went on at the 'shop' was interesting.

His ruminations were rudely shattered by the appearance of his wife and daughter.

'Do you want this thing on?'

Without waiting for an answer, Vera switched the set off. Betty Bolam muttered a subdued 'hello' and they all sat at the table in silence.

Vera was the first to break it. 'You said you'd mend that plug on the landing – it's not done yet. I can't use the Hoover,' she said accusingly.

'I can't do it in the dark, can I? – I'll have to turn the power off. It'll have to wait till Saturday afternoon. Anyway, I told you, I've got to go out tonight.'

Betty went a shade whiter around the mouth. She was a slim, pale girl and her blanched cheeks made her hair and eyes all the darker by contrast. She stared at her plate, then spoke. 'You – you're not going round the clubs again tonight?'

Alec stared at her grimly. 'I am indeed – what about it?'

She gulped, but said nothing.

Her father thumped the table with his fist. 'I spoke to you, miss … by some chance, are you thinking of going to a certain club as well? Is that it?' His voice rose to a shout.

Betty burst into tears. She jumped from the table and ran from the room.

As her daughter's feet hammered up the stairs, Vera Bolam went into action. 'You've done it again. Why don't you mind your own business?' she hissed. 'If she wants to go out with King Kong, that's up to her. You damned, interfering …'

He wasn't listening. Striding out into the hall, he looked up the stairs, then stamped up after his daughter. She had locked her bedroom door by the time he got there. He thumped on the thin panels, before putting his face to them. 'Listen, my girl, just because you've got your mother on your side, you needn't think it will make any difference. You may be twenty-one now, but you'll get fixed up with that layabout over my dead body, and by God, I mean that!'

There was a fresh outburst of sobbing from inside.

'He's no good, Betty. If he's up to what I think, he'll be before the court before long. And then you can do your courting on visiting days in Durham jail!' He listened again. 'D'you hear me, then?'

There was no reply and he came slowly down the stairs,

baffled. At the bottom, his wife stood waiting, her hands on her hips. She said nothing, only looked at him with almost a pitying hatred. He brushed past her into the lounge and stood glowering in the middle of the carpet. She followed him in.

'Come on then, say it,' he snapped. 'Why don't I mind my own business? Look, Vera, if you knew that fellow like I do – knew his sort, the types he mixes with … twitchy with pep pills, and making pin money flogging his spare ones around the town.'

She still said nothing, just looked at him. Sitting down at the table, she began sipping her cup of tea.

Alec rounded on her. 'All right, stay dumb – I'm off!' He tore out of the room, grabbed his coat from the hall and stormed out to the car.

Chapter Six

While Alec Bolam was cursing himself towards the city, equally harsh words were being spoken by other policemen at The Quayside in Newcastle.

The tide was low and so getting the body up from the police launch to the wharf was no easy job. The light was poor and, in spite of plenty of available muscles, the rocking boat and steep wooden piles made the raising of the green canvas stretcher a difficult job.

With much panting and grunting, the literally 'dead' weight was finally brought over the edge of the Quayside. In the darkness it was trotted over the cobbles to the archaic public mortuary and they just managed to squeeze the stretcher through the door of the tiny Victorian relic, which would have just about housed a car with no room to spare. When the police cars arrived, the tiny building was soon packed to suffocation with large men.

The smallest figure was the one who was to hold the centre of the stage, Dr John Ellison. He clawed his way across to a row of hooks and hung his clothes up. Then he pulled on a wrinkled gown and plastic apron which he produced from a bag, together with some surgical instruments.

MacDonald loomed up at the end of the antique porcelain table in the middle of the room. With him was Detective Superintendent Potts, his second-in-command at the CID, and the DI of the Tyne Division.

'Let's be having a bit of space; anyone not having any real business here, clear off out.'

A clear zone appeared reluctantly around the slab and

the pathologist, together with the arty-looking man from the laboratory, stood alongside as Milburn and a PC unstrapped the stretcher and laid the body on the table.

'Still a canny bit of mud on him,' observed the Tyne DI.

The next few minutes were spent in cleaning up and taking yet more photographs, the cameramen moaning all the time that there were no proper power points for their floodlights.

When their dust had settled, Gasgoine Burke carefully removed the wire loops from the ankles and wrists. 'I've cut them at the sides, Super, to keep the "knots" intact – they were twisted three or four times in the front.'

The wires, severed by pliers, were reverently laid on clean brown paper and carefully labelled as exhibits.

'What happened to the ends, d'ye think?' asked the Scotsman.

Burke delicately brushed back his floppy hair with the back of his hand. 'Recent fractures, on all four ends. They'd been twisted badly at the point of breakage. I'd say they'd been rotated back and forth for some time, then finally snapped.'

'Think they had weights on them?'

'Quite probably – the swaying of the body in the tide must have weakened the wires and the final grabbing by the dredger buckets has snapped them right off.

Meanwhile Ellison had been looking at the wreckage of the face. 'The bucket hit him there all right – he's had a devil of a clout. Not a hope of identifying him by his features.'

Some of the less hardy souls tried to avoid looking too directly at the face, but MacDonald had got used to it and stared at the mess with interest. 'What can you tell us about him, Doc? He looks a fairly young man, somehow.'

John Ellison had been busy with a steel tape-measure. 'Five feet eight, slim build, be about ten and a half stone,

I'd guess. Young adult, pretty good teeth – those that are left. Hair sort of gingery blond. Certainly no baldness, though the front part of the scalp has been torn away.'

He was looking at the fingers now.

'Hard to tell much, with all this washerwoman's wrinkling, but they don't look like the fingers of a man doing hard manual labour. Have a job getting prints from these fingers, but it may be the only way you'll get a definite identification.'

He prodded about in the horror of the face and finally decided that the eyes had been blue. 'No tattoos or operation scars – in fact, a dead loss from the identification point of view. No fillings or extractions in the teeth, either.'

He took time off to record all this into a small portable tape machine.

The small room began to warm up from the sheer fug of policeman's perspiration and cigarette smoke, and two of the photographers eventually decided that they would rather suffer the cold night air than the sordid atmosphere inside. They stood at the door, lighting cigarettes and gazing over the cluster of police vehicles to the lights up on the Tyne Bridge.

Presently there was a bellow from inside and the Tyne DI stuck his head out. 'They want some more photos, so come and hold up your dicky birds.'

Inside, the pathologist had started on the inside of the body and had an assortment of fractures and bruises to be recorded on film and tape.

'He's broken his neck – that's the actual cause of death,' said Ellison to MacDonald later. 'Apart from that, he's had a fair old battering. Four broken ribs, a haemorrhage around one kidney and a hell of a clout on the back of the head.'

The chief superintendent rubbed his own cadaverous chin. 'All caused before death?' he asked.

Ellison bobbed his head, rather curtly. 'Of course. He also had seven bad bruises on his chest and side, tallying with the damage around his kidney and some of the rib fractures. My guess is that someone put the boot into him.'

'What about the broken neck?'

'Looks as if he's had his head cracked against something. No fracture of the skull, but the bruising on the front of the brain shows that he's fallen backwards on to something hard – that's how his neck was broken.'

Potts, the Headquarters man, looked ruminatively at the wreckage of the dead man's face. 'All that mess was done after death?'

Ellison nodded. 'All post-mortem injuries – he'd probably been in the water a couple of days before that happened. The water is damned cold at this time of year, but a bit of decomposition has started on the stomach wall.'

MacDonald jumped on this. 'So what's the likely time of death?'

Ellison began peeling the grubby gown from his tubby figure. 'Very hard to say … more than two to three days, less than ten. I'm only guessing. Damned impossible to be at all accurate,' he added with a sudden outburst of petulance.

MacDonald turned to the drooping figure of Gasgoine Burke. 'Can you help us any more, Mr Burke?'

The young man shrugged. 'No clothes, no damn all – only a couple of bits of wire!' He sniffed disdainfully. 'Forensic-wise, this is about the most sterile murder we've had. Can't expect much trace evidence, after swilling about naked in the Tyne for days.'

The Scots detective looked more dyspeptic than ever. 'What have we got, then? … a dead man, definitely murdered, gingery-fair hair, five foot eight, age …' He looked across at the pathologist who was struggling back into his outer clothes. 'Any nearer age, Doc?'

Ellison paused, one fat arm jammed in a sleeve. 'More than twenty to twenty-three – all his wisdom teeth are through. The seams in his skull bones suggest he's less than thirty-five. That's the best I can do for you. If it turns out to be important, we'll have to organize some X-rays of his bones, but that'll be a hell of fag in a place like this.'

MacDonald got on with his inventory of facts, while Potts made some quick notes in his pocket book. 'OK. Twenty to thirty-five. No distinguishing marks at all.' Potts looked up quickly from his book. 'What about fingerprints, sir? If he's got "form", that's our best bet to get identification.'

Uncle Mac looked across at the sergeant who dealt with 'dabs'. So far, he'd had to stand by in frustrated inaction. 'Any hopes?' asked MacDonald.

'Not in the present state, sir. I'll take those and see what can be done with them overnight.'

'Those' were a line of ten little bottles, each containing a carefully labelled fingertip from the body.

'Useless trying to get prints from them while they're waterlogged, I'll try injecting glycerine into them and perhaps formalin if that fails.'

The chief superintendent nodded at him. 'Do your best as soon as possible. If you can roll them first thing in the morning, send them down to NECRO[1] by car. If they can't help, we'll have to try the Yard, but God knows how long that will take.'

Potts broke in again. 'About missing persons, sir … I checked an hour ago – nothing reported on Tyneside in the last week that would remotely resemble this fellow. Mostly young girls, in fact.'

The CID chief's face became grimmer still. 'Let's pray that he's got a criminal record then.'

There was a slow exodus towards the door, but Mac

---

[1] North East Criminal Records Office.

suddenly pulled up. 'Where's that sergeant from the Tyne? Ah, Milburn, isn't it? Look, where do you think a body would have to go into the river to end up where it did'

The River officer thought for a moment. 'Not very far away, sir, if he was weighted down. I'd say it would have to have gone in along the quarter-mile stretch between Albert Edward Dock and the ferry landing.'

MacDonald nodded. 'But certainly on that side of the river?'

'Aye, certainly, sir … there's no cross current to speak of from one bank to t'other.'

MacDonald looked at Potts. 'So it looks very likely that he was thrown in on the North side – the Newcastle side.'

The superintendent agreed. 'And you think it more likely that his killers came from there, rather than the Gateshead-South Shields side?'

'Seems more likely,' said the old Scot, 'Though they might be extra cunning and come from a hell of a distance off, like Teesside or even one of the big Yorkshire towns. Wouldn't be the first time that a body's been brought up to the Tyne for dumping.'

The drift to the door started again and the theorizing continued as the different groups dispersed, some back to Headquarters and others slipping off for a crafty glass of beer.

A few minutes later, Alec Bolam heard the latest on the murder as the Headquarters contingent arrived back, but he still had no inkling that it was soon to join up with his own troubles.

The final scenes of that eventful day were played out in the Rising Sun Club in the Bigg Market.

Jackie Stott stood with his Danish manager just inside the room on the first floor. The stripper was writhing her last few sequins off on to the floor and four perspiring musicians were hammering out the 'bumps and grinds' for her as a hundred pairs of eyes goggled over the brims of tankards and glasses.

The two men stood at the back of the room while the girl finished her act amid ragged applause. There was no curtain to fall on the climax of her nudity, so she had evolved a routine of having a large red satin cloak flung around her by a helpful Freddie, who leaned over from the dais to settle it around her shoulders. As she ran off to the diminutive dressing room, the two men moved back towards the doors and made their way up to the gaming room above.

'This new croupier seems good – the one from Sheffield,' observed the Dane. 'Losing Geordie Armstrong was inconvenient at the moment, having to send Arthur down to the boat from here.'

Jackie looked covertly at the speaker. *If only you knew, lad*, he thought.

Aloud, he said, 'Try and get another. Geordie'll not be back. He's taken off for good; his digs are empty.'

He didn't say how he came to know. Thor kept his face as straight as ever, but he promised Jackie a surprise over the matter of young Armstrong.

Upstairs, the wheels were spinning merrily and several card games were going on with full tables. Jackie enjoyed this room the most and settled down for a night's patrol up there. Downstairs could look after itself, with the able supervision of his manager.

A sudden thought struck him. 'Where's Laura?' Perhaps it was a symptom of their relationship that he hadn't missed her before.

'She's in your flat – said she had a headache and was going to put her feet up between her numbers,' replied the Dane.

Stott grunted, but the thought somehow unsettled him. She should be out here, with him. He wanted to stalk around with her in tow, showing her off as his personal bird – why the hell should she skulk inside – was she ashamed of being seen with him all of a sudden?

Too damn big for her high heels, is Laura lately, he glowered. But he shook off his sudden black mood and noticed Joe Blunt lurking in a corner of the room. He was due back at the *Mississippi* soon; it opened much later than the Rising Sun, catering for the hard core of gamblers, who were willing to stay up most of the night. Joe came up to the Bigg Market every night to collect the large cash 'float' to distribute to the three croupiers down on the river boat.

'All OK down there, Joe?' grunted Jackie, winking at him.

Joe nodded lugubriously, his slack mouth working. Neither he nor Jackie had seen the evening paper nor heard the radio or TV about the finding of a body in the Tyne that afternoon.

Jackie patted the old pug's massive arm. 'Time you got back, Joe. Keep it quiet tonight, eh – no mixing it with the coppers!'

They both guffawed. Jackie's anger over the incident on the previous Saturday had become submerged in the big secret they thought they alone shared.

He had made another circuit or two of the casino, nodded regally to the regular patrons and wondered more and more where Laura was – damn her and her headache! He suddenly spat his cigar into the nearest ashtray and headed for the door of his flat.

In the lounge, he found his mistress lying on the settee with a glass in her hand and her shoes on the floor.

'What's wrong, hinny – the club too low-class for you these nights?'

She scowled up at him. 'Don't start needling me, Jackie – I'm not in the mood.'

The sight of her lying there languidly, 'all legs and bosom' as he coarsely thought of it, touched off something deep inside him. 'You're a bloody fine woman, Laura,' he muttered thickly, going around the settee, and dropping on to his knees alongside her.

She tried to squirm out of his way, but his powerful arms pinned her to the cushions as his lips clamped over hers. Wriggling violently, Laura tried to pull free, but Jackie was roused too far by now. He gradually let his weight settle on her and, by keeping his mouth on hers, prevented her from spitting out the choice language that was obviously fermenting inside her. His hand fumbled to the zip between her shoulders, which set off another paroxysm of jerking. He let his lips slide down to kiss her neck.

'Get off – get off me, you dirty old bastard!' she gasped, the weight of his chest making speech difficult. 'Go and rape – the bloody – barmaid – will you!'

He lifted his mouth momentarily to grate in her ear, 'Don't get so high and mighty, Edna Dodds. Don't forget that crummy place in Doncaster, hinny – maybe they'd like you back.'

He kissed her again roughly, stemming her foul language, then took on a more wheedling tone. 'Come on, love, you haven't been around nights for weeks – let's have a bit of fun, like the old days, eh?'

Her answer was to try to remove the lobe of one of his ears with her talon-like fingernails.

He grunted with pain. 'You bitch – if you're thinking your precious boyfriend is still around, have another think! You won't be seeing him again.'

Her eyes widened and she pushed frantically against his chest. 'What the hell to you mean?' she gasped.

He laughed nastily. 'Darling Geordie – you've had him, sweet … "finito", get it?'

She dropped back in relief and laughed sarcastically. 'You silly damned fool, Jackie! What the hell do I care about Geordie Armstrong. Not whether he's alive or damn well dead!'

There was a sudden hammering on the door. The sound of a key in the outer lock and another frantic tapping on the lounge door heralded Herbert Lumley.

Jackie struggled off the settee and furiously brushed himself down. 'What the hell d'yer mean, barging in like that?' he snarled.

The old soldier had never done such a thing before but from the look of him, some emergency was stirring him up. 'Sorry, Mr Stott, but can you come down at once. I don't like the look of what's going on, not at all I don't!'

The normally serene doorman was more agitated than Jackie had ever seen him. The club owner's anger rapidly cooled off and he came across the room to Herbert, as Laura flounced to the mirror to tidy herself up.

Herbert had already turned to lead the way downstairs. 'Two men, sir, foreign types. Barges in without membership cards. I tried to stop them, but one stamped on me foot. When I grabbed him, the other pulled a knife on me.'

Jackie took a deep breath. 'We'll soon sort them out, Herb. Where's Hansen?'

'Downstairs, keeping an eye on them. I tipped him the wink when they forced past me. They went across to the bar.'

The Rising Sun had had its fair share of hoodlums and layabouts, but Herbert Lumley's hidden muscles, occasionally helped by Jackie's prominent ones, kept the place clear without much trouble. No one had ever pulled a knife in there before, but there had to be a first time, Jackie thought, as he followed the old army man down the stairs. The recent inflation of his own troubleshooting image, over the Armstrong affair, made him even more confident that these two characters wouldn't last half a minute.

They stopped inside the swing-doors and stared around the big room.

'That's them, in the middle.'

Herbert pointed an indignant finger at a table at the edge of the dance floor, opposite the band. All Jackie could see was the back of two stocky, thick-necked men. They had a glass apiece and Herbert anticipated Jackie's first complaint. 'The bar staff wouldn't know there was any trouble, sir. They serve anybody once they're inside.'

Jackie scowled. 'Then they'd better sup up bloody fast … in about five seconds flat.'

He rolled menacingly across the room towards them, noticing on the way that Thor Hansen was watching warily from the end of the bar. Stott loomed up at the table and glowered down at the two newcomers.

'You blokes got membership cards?' he grated.

A pair of swarthy faces looked up at him insolently. One man, with oily black hair and thin moustache, flashed gold-capped teeth as he spoke. 'You the big man, I suppose – siddown, have one of your drinks.'

There was such calculated insult in the strongly accented words that Jackie almost took a swipe at him.

'Listen, Gonzales, or whatever you call yourself – get off your arse and beat it – and take your organ-grinder's monkey with you!'

He jerked a thumb at the other intruder, a slightly smaller man but with the same dark skin and glossy black hair. Neither of them spoke for a moment, but looked at each other and smiled falsely.

'These mugs in the provinces live in a little world of their own, Bruno,' said the first, sweetly.

The smaller, hard-faced man nodded back. 'Almost a pity to disturb them, Kostas – but better try to educate them before we get accused of exploiting them.'

Jackie was rapidly going purple with rage. 'Get out, before I smash your heads together,' he hissed. He thumped the table with a great fist and one of the glasses toppled over, spilling whisky over the trouser leg of the man called Bruno.

So fast that Stott saw no movement, Bruno had the point of a knife pressed against Jackie's wrist. More from surprise than fear, he stood motionless, watching it for a few seconds.

People on nearby tables began to notice the trouble and started to shuffle uneasily.

The older man, the one called Kostas, tapped his friend's arm. 'Wait a few minutes, Bruno ... we'd better go somewhere and have a little talk in private, Mr Stott. We wouldn't like your customers to be disturbed, would we, Bruno? You might lose some business and that wouldn't do any of us any good, would it?'

The two Levantine-looking gents laughed together cynically. The knife vanished. Jackie was in two minds whether or not to annihilate them with a couple of blows from his fists, but the penny dropped with their last few words. 'Protection boys,' he muttered to himself. *Protection be damned, but what was the best way to teach them a lesson?*

As he hesitated, Herbert appeared at his elbow, having seen the knife appear again.

'Shall I phone for the police, Mr Stott?'

The two intruders looked at each other again and guffawed.

Jackie towered over them, boiling with rage, but anxious not to disturb the patrons.

'No, leave it,' he snapped. 'Has Joe gone?'

'Just this minute.'

'Get after him and tell him to get back here at the double. There may be some rubbish for him to scrape off the floor.' He crooked a finger at the two men. 'I'll give you one minute in the office – then I'm going to kick you down the stairs.'

Stott stood back while they got leisurely up from their chairs. He pointed in the direction of the foyer, being careful to follow them, not lead the way. Thor Hansen unobtrusively joined the procession which filed out to the tiny office, watched by many curious eyes.

Thor squeezed last into the cubicle and shut the door.

'Don't sit down – you're not stopping,' rasped Jackie sarcastically. He leant against a filing cabinet. 'Who are you and what d'yer bloody want – and you're not getting it, that's for a start!' he snapped contemptuously.

The older, more burly, Greek calmly fitted a cigarette into a black holder. 'I am Kostas Papagos and this is my business associate, Bruno Casella,' he began. 'As I said outside, you country bumpkins up in the North don't know what makes the world go round, so we've taken the trouble to come and wise you up – before some objectionable characters get ahead of us.'

Jackie sighed. 'And how much did you hope to get, *Antonio*?'

Papagos frowned, but kept up the polite charade by turning to his partner. 'Perhaps they're not so primitive after all, Bruno – he seems to have caught on to the idea all right.' Turning back to Jackie, he said, 'For a mere hundred a week, we guarantee complete insurance.'

'Against what?'

The Greek shrugged and spread his palms out in an all-embracing gesture. 'Everything – except bad weather! Mainly against accidental breakages, loss of custom and fire damage,' he added sarcastically.

Jackie Stott's eyes glinted. He had wanted to hear their story to make sure – now he felt he had their measure. 'That all you got to say? You're the mouthpiece, Papagos – don't your monkey here have a tongue of his own?'

Casella went white and his knife hand twitched. Papagos's fixed leer faded a little and he spoke softly. 'Don't be too clever, Stott – we like our little joke and you can have yours, but don't push your luck too far. Bruno here is a man of action, not words.'

The ex-boxer, who stood half a head over both of them, stuck his head out pugnaciously. 'Well I got some words now, see. You London yobs think you can ride anybody, especially us *yokels* in the provinces … well, you can stop right here, see!' He lurched forward from the desk where he had been lounging, making Papagos start back slightly. 'You can stuff your bloody protection where the kangaroos keep their keys … Now I'm going to throw you both out and if you so much as let your shadow fall on mine again, I'll kill the pair of yee … I ain't particular about who I croak, as long as I don't get my hands dirty!'

Unwisely, he couldn't resist the final bragging about fatal disposal of his enemies. Thor dropped another piece of his mental jigsaw into place as he watched warily from the doorway.

The whimsical mask fell from Papagos's face. 'We'll see, Stott – we'll see. If that's how you want it, we'll have to arrange a little demonstration, eh, Bruno? Nothing like showing a customer how a thing works when you want to break down sales resistance.'

He made for the door, with Casella in tow. Thor jerked it open and stood aside to let them through and, as Papagos passed him, the slightest of winks passed between them.

As he neared the outer door Papagos lost his false smile for good. 'You're doing the wrong thing, Jackie boy,' he said. 'You're going to be so very sorry.'

Before he could make a sufficiently offensive reply, Jackie heard the thump of feet on the stairs. The doors erupted inwards and a panting Joe Blunt burst in, followed by Herbert Lumley.

Joe took one look at the two foreigners and threw himself on them, like a trusty bulldog coming to the aid of 'Little Master'. His battered face looked like some demented lion as he swung them round and began dragging them towards the stairs.

Jackie stood back grinning. 'That's it, Joe – fling 'em out. If you ever see their ugly mugs again, you got my full permission to separate 'em from their teeth!'

The pair of them made no resistance apart from threats as the old sparring partner hustled them down to the street.

Jackie followed to see them off the premises and caught the last words of Papagos as Joe sent them reeling across the pavement with a final push.

'You'll be sorry, Stott – we'll make an example of you and your damned club – one Newcastle won't forget.'

'Aw, get stuffed!' yelled Jackie, as he patted Joe's leviathan shoulder.

They turned and walked upstairs, where Thor Hansen met them with a slight frown creasing his usually impassive face.

'No one mucks me about, lad,' said Jackie smugly. 'That's the last we'll hear of them yobs.'

Hansen knew better and looked calculatingly at his watch.

Chapter Seven

An hour later, Laura Levine sat at the bar of the Rising Sun with Thor Hansen.

Freda, the barmaid, had exchanged her usual icy looks with the singer and had pointedly moved away as far as possible.

'Jackie's upstairs, watching the wheel, so we can talk in peace for a minute.' Laura sounded angry and dispirited.

'Things are moving, darling – faster than you think,' murmured the handsome Dane, his eyes intent on the tonic he was adding to her gin.

'About time – I tell you, Thor, I've had about enough of that common swine.' She gulped some of her drink almost desperately. 'You've got to do something about us, Thor – and quick. I can't take much more of this.'

Hansen tapped her hand placatingly. 'It's all working out fine – that little affair tonight will hurry it on.'

She shook her head emphatically. 'It's got to be now. He's turning nasty.'

He squeezed her fingers, then drew back his hand discreetly. 'All right, darling – I'll have another word with Papagos and see if he can bring things to a head more quickly.'

He hesitated, as if unsure of how much he should tell.

'There's something else, Laura, something that would clinch it, but I don't think that I should tell you just yet.'

Laura leaned forward eagerly. 'What is it? Come on, for God's sake, don't go telling half-truths and then leaving them.'

He shook his head stubbornly. 'No, I shouldn't have

said anything. But I wanted you to know that I've got it all worked out.'

He refused to be drawn in spite of her persuasion and she was left with a tantalizing mystery.

'Whatever it is, Thor, make it quick! I want us to get on the level, not behind Jackie's back – we can even get married.'

He nodded and furtively squeezed her hand again, wondering how he was going to break the news that he had a wife in Copenhagen, though he hadn't seen her for eight years. His habitual poker face hid a turbulent, scheming mind, with ambition as its main driving force.

Laura looked at him speculatively. 'You knew these wops when you were in London?'

Thor nodded. 'They have a grip on one section of the Soho clubs – including the place I managed before I came here.'

'And yet you got on all right with them?'

She sounded dubious.

'You have to be protected by someone down there, darling – if it hadn't been them, it would be some other gang. Better to pay up and let them fight your battles, than commit suicide, like Jackie did tonight.'

Laura bit her lip. 'They won't hurt him – physically, I mean?'

He shrugged. 'Perhaps not, if he plays sensibly from now on. But if he keeps on acting stubborn, he may get a better beating than he can hand out.'

'He seems to have changed in the last few days,' went on the singer, slightly maudlin now, with a few drinks inside her. 'He's so cocky, as if he's done something marvellous … throwing himself around like some cheap gangster.'

Thor patted the back of her hand. 'That's all part of this affair I hinted at. He's going to fall with a big crash soon and I wouldn't want you to go down with him.'

She sighed and glanced at her diamante wristwatch.

'Nearly time for my next number – God, if you knew how I hate these gawping idiots!'

Adjusting the neckline of her dress to show even more white flesh, she glanced about the club to see if the boys from the band were preparing to get back to the platform. Her eyes fixed on Freddie, sitting at a nearby table. 'Lover-girl is back again, I see,' she commented.

Thor Hansen turned his head to see Alex Bolam's daughter sitting with the guitar player. 'Her old man has never been in here at the same time,' he mused. 'I wonder if that's deliberate.'

Laura's heavily mascaraed eyes opened wider.

'Here's your chance to find out, sweet – here's the old man himself!'

The tall figure of Alec Bolam appeared just inside the glass doors. He had thrown his hat on Herbert's counter outside and strode in to the club room, his eyes picking out his daughter at once. He materialized above the couple as the manager and singer watched with interest from the bar.

Freddie looked up in guilty surprise, then rose to his feet and stared from father to daughter with nervous uncertainty.

Laura and the Dane could hear none of the words, but from the drawn expression on the girl's face and the grim scowl on that of the detective, they guessed that no pleasantries were being swapped.

'What d'you want – why are you following me?' Betty's voice was low and tense.

'I'm here on business – as you well know. I want you out of here, there may be trouble.'

She looked up quickly. 'And you're going to make it, I suppose?'

He shook his head. 'Not this time – another sort of trouble. Nothing to do with you – or even him,' he added contemptuously, looking at the uneasy Freddie, for the first time.

'I – I'd better be off, love – time for Laura's number.' His loose mouth twitched nervously.

Alec Bolam glared at him. 'Better take another purple heart, Freddie – your nerves are showing!'

Freddie gulped and backed away, then hurried to the rostrum.

Betty Bolam watched him go, her fists clenched tightly. She swung back to her father and spoke with suppressed violence. 'Satisfied? You can't leave anyone alone, can you! You spoilt Mum's life, now you're starting on mine!'

Bolam suddenly dropped into the vacant chair and ran an anguished hand through his hair. 'Look, Betty – try and understand for once. I promised your mother not to come the heavy hand with you, but that yob – he's no good, love.' He bent forward and his voice was cracking with the intensity of his feelings. 'It's my job to stop people acting like he does. It's my job, pet,' he ended almost in a whisper.

She glared back, stony-faced. 'And your pleasure, too!'

Alec swung his head, wearily. 'Pleasure! Good God, Betty, can't you see my life's hell? Your mother … oh, forget it.' He changed his tack abruptly and his voice became brisker and harder. 'Now let's have some sense. I want you out of here, straight away. Nothing to do with him. There's going to be trouble in this place – maybe tonight, maybe tomorrow – but soon.'

Impressed by the authority of his tone, she looked him in the face. 'What sort of trouble?'

He shrugged. 'Two big-time protection racket men from London have been seen in Newcastle tonight. One of the men on the beat saw them being chucked out of here earlier on – there'll be fireworks before long, take it from me. So I want you out – and if you won't go quietly, I'll carry you out, so make your choice.'

This time she knew he was telling the truth. 'I was going, anyway – I never stay when Freddie's got to work for a long time.' She pushed her chair back and stood up.

'I'll take you home,' offered her father.

'I thought you were busy this time of night.'

Her voice was still cold and uncompromising.

'I can come back.'

She was just going to brush him off, when chaos hit the big room.

A loud crash made Bolam spin around. He was just in time to see the last fragments of glass tumble from the main window that overlooked the Bigg Market. Something rolled on to the floor a few yards from the detective and immediately burst into flames. Luckily, most of the patrons were at tables around the walls or at the bar and no one was actually sitting where the bomb landed. But yells and screams filled the room and the music died away into a discordant drone. A sheet of yellow flame leapt up as a flammable liquid gushed over the floor and soaked into the carpet. Clouds of acrid black smoke billowed above it and within seconds the yells turned to coughing. The surrounding tables were overturned as people trampled around in terror. The flames licked wider and wider across the floor, though the actual area involved was much smaller than panic-stricken customers imagined.

Bolam was one of those who acted first. He grabbed his daughter around the shoulders and hustled her towards the doors, slightly ahead of the general stampede. 'Get out – get a taxi home.' He gave her a shove in the back and then ran to a red fire extinguisher hanging on the wall.

Herbert Lumley, the only other with any presence of mind, dashed in from the foyer with another and within seconds the two men were dousing the floor and tables with jets of fizzing soda-acid foam. The next to take action was Thor Hansen, though Laura noticed that he deliberately waited a few seconds before moving to get an extinguisher.

In spite of the terrifying initial fireball, the flames died quickly. The bomb was a beer flagon filled with paraffin, a length of colliery fuse stuck in the neck. It had been deliberately designed to create fear and disturbance rather than to burn down the Rising Sun. If it had been filled with petrol, the result might have been different.

The three jets of foam soon isolated and then extinguished the flames but, inside two minutes, the room was a smoky, smut-filled shambles. A heaving mass was now jostling to get through the foyer to the stairs, and Herbert had to leave his fire-fighting to attend to his besieged cloakroom counter.

In the middle of this pandemonium, Jackie Stott raced downstairs from the gaming room and stood raving in the centre of the main club. The arrival of the fire brigade a moment later made the confusion more devastating, as uniformed men battled up the narrow staircase against the down-going tide of outraged ex-patrons.

The fire Section Officer advanced on the fuming club owner. 'Good work on the part of your men, sir – nothing much left for us to do, except investigate the cause and call the police.'

Jackie stopped short in the middle of his apoplectic tirade. 'Police! What the hell do we want the police for? … it's just a fire. Keep the coppers out of this!'

The fire officer smiled indulgently. 'Now, sir, be reasonable. This was no ordinary fire – somebody threw a bomb through your window – the person who rang up with the alarm said so, and the stink of paraffin and that broken window confirms it … here it is, what's left of it.'

A helmeted fireman handed him the broken neck of a brown bottle, a piece of hollow fuse still held in position with putty.

Alec Bolam had padded up behind them. 'Who wants the police? We're already here – were here even before it happened!'

Jackie Stott almost foamed at the mouth. 'Bombs! Firemen! … And now damn police walking all over me! Haven't I got enough trouble with all this?'

He swept a hand around the rapidly emptying room but, at that very moment, three uniformed policemen battled their way into the club. One was a sergeant from the local beat, the other two were from a motor patrol that followed the fire tender.

The sergeant advanced on them, picking his way through the overturned chairs. He saw Bolam and touched his blue and white banded cap. 'What's happened, sir?'

'Somebody "arson" about, sergeant,' punned Bolam with grim humour. 'No casualties, thank goodness. You'd better catch some of those clients and try to get a few statements, though half of 'em have shoved off by now. And I can't say I blame them!'

He gave the infuriated Stott a mirthless smile.

'Better close up, Jackie – you'll do no more business tonight. I'll bet all your mugs upstairs have slung their hook by now – they may be afraid that your wop friends may come back with an H-bomb next time!'

Rage faded to astonishment on the ex-boxer's face. *How the hell did Bolam know about the visit of Papagos and Casella so quickly?*

Bolam turned back to the uniformed sergeant. 'I'd better run this for the time being – call up the station on your joy-box there and tell them what's happened. Ask them to rout out Jimmy Grainger and get him to phone me here.'

He looked at the two mobile men. 'Give the sergeant a hand in rounding up some customers and the staff – start taking statements, I suppose. A waste of time, but we've got to go through the motions.'

The sergeant pulled out his small personal radio that was clipped inside his coat, extended the aerial and called up the Central Police Station to relay a message to Information Room.

'Better tell them to notify Chief Superintendent MacDonald, too,' added Bolam, 'though I expect he's still busy with that murder.'

Jackie Stott pricked up his ears. The mention of murder struck a sensitive spot.

He had a bigger shock coming.

Bolam, genuinely unaware of Stott's interest, made another of his jibes at the club owner. 'Better watch yourself, Jackie … this time it was a home-made bomb. Next time, we may be dragging you out of the Tyne with your legs lashed together!'

Jackie went as pale as a corpse himself. His mind whirled as he tried to grasp what Bolam had said. A body from the river – legs tied together! *They must have found Geordie already*! *God, what the hell am I to do*!

He looked around wildly, almost on the point of making a run for it. In a moment the ex-fighter had got control of himself again. Bolam hadn't said it was Geordie Armstrong, though it was unlikely that there were two murdered bodies in the river at the same time.

'I need a drink,' he muttered. 'Where's Hansen?'

He stumbled across to the deserted bar, poured himself a triple whisky and threw it down neat.

The uniformed policemen had started to round up the stragglers and had herded them to some tables in the far corner of the room. The firemen had gone, except the section officer and another senior man who had just arrived.

Bolam checked with the sergeant that nothing had been seen of the bomb-throwers from outside, then went over to the long figure of Jackie Stott at the bar.

'Right, now let's have your version of it, Jackie … I know Papagos and Casella have been in here … and I don't need twenty questions to guess what they wanted!'

The club owner stared fixedly at the glass-backed shelves behind the bar.

'I got nothing to say, copper,' he muttered.

Alec Bolam sighed. 'No use coming the dumb act, Jackie … you're in real trouble now. For once I give you credit for flinging those London yobs out. Though I'm sure that you didn't do it just to please me!' The sarcastic banter came back into his voice.

Stott was only half-listening to the detective – the bomb incident was submerged in the far greater peril of the finding of Armstrong's body. If only this damn copper would stop jabbering and give him time to think – to work out what to do! He had to find out more about it for his own sake – but he could hardly ask the man standing alongside him.

Bolam, all unsuspecting of Stott's fearful anxiety, pressed him again about the fracas in the club. 'They did this to you as a gentle warning, Jackie – if that had been petrol instead of paraffin, we'd be out in the street now, watching it all burn down.'

There was no answer.

'Come on, man – how much did Papagos want? Give us a statement and we'll have them inside before morning. They couldn't hurt you then. We'll have a "demanding with menaces" charge on 'em, if only you'll cough.'

Stott continued to glare at the back of the bar.

Bolam tried wheedling. 'Jackie, look, you know damn fine what a pair of villains they are – the boys in the Met could have had them half a dozen times if they could have witnesses to testify against them.'

Stott swung round at this.

'And why couldn't they get witnesses, eh? Because they'd have had their throats cut or their wives maimed before they got halfway to court … be your age, Bolam, I'm going to play this my way.'

Before the detective could begin to argue again, the

sergeant came over. 'Grainger is on the blower for you, sir – over there.' He pointed to a coin box under a soundproof hood that was intended for the use of patrons.

Alec went across and picked up the receiver.

'That you, Jimmy … things are moving … yes, a bomb through the window … no kidding! Look, try to pick up Papagos and Casella. Just ask them if they'd like to answer a few questions. No, we can't make them, but I'll bet they've blown already, so it won't arise. They'll have an alibi like the Tower of London, but we've got to try. Where? … God knows, halfway back to Soho is my guess by now.' He listened for a moment. 'Then chase up any rogues who might have done this for Papagos – check stolen car lists after nine o'clock. No point in coming round here – Stott won't cough and we can't do much without a statement or a complaint from him … this will only be the start, I reckon.'

He rang off just as more police and the photography and fingerprint men arrived. For a few minutes he talked with the staff and the few patrons that the uniformed men had managed to detain. No one knew any more than Bolam himself.

The remains of the bomb were carefully collected for the forensic laboratory.

A few minutes later, Joe Blunt blundered up the stairs. One of the croupiers had phoned him with the news of the firebomb and he had come back as fast as a taxi would bring him. Jackie came out of his worried paralysis at the bar and hustled him upstairs to the flat. Laura had disappeared and Thor Hansen was running the liaison with the police, such as it was.

Upstairs, Jackie clutched the old pug's arm as soon as the door of the flat closed behind them. 'Joe, they've found Geordie's body already. What the hell are we going to do?'

Joe gaped uncomprehendingly. 'They can't have – we wired half a hundredweight of old iron on to him!'

'Well, they bloody well have! It's been on the news and the telly, so Herbert Lumley said just now. Half the coppers in Newcastle are on the job – and the other half are downstairs, by the looks of it.' He shakily poured a couple of whiskies and swallowed one at a gulp. 'Help yourself … the hell of it is, we can't ask outright what's going on. When's the next news on the radio?'

Joe shrugged. 'Too late now for local news – hev te wait till papers in the morning.'

He had too little imagination to realize what danger he was in. He sheltered mentally behind Jackie and, as long as his boss was around, that was enough to reassure him.

Stott tore open his collar button and pulled the knot of his tie down for comfort.

'Not knowing anything is what kills me. Can't even ask Thor Hansen on this one. He's the boy for problems, but not when it's a murder.'

Joe blinked his piggy eyes. 'Reckon he's got a big enough problem of his own downstairs – what's bin happening?'

Jackie looked at the old sparring partner gloomily and poured another drink. 'Those London mobsters – quick off the mark. But we'll fix them, if we can get round this other business all right … everything bloody well comes at once.'

'What about the coppers … how they taking this?'

'They know the score about Papagos – God knows how. They'd like to see him played off against me, so that we'd both go down. But they're going to be unlucky. I'll handle this myself!'

Some of the old bravado began to return as the alcohol seeped through his system.

There was a silence as Joe slowly digested the facts.

'What we going to do about it all, then?' he asked

eventually.

'Where Geordie is concerned – sit tight. As far as I can see, they don't know who he is yet, or they'd have been round here as fast as their little feet could carry them.' He brightened up a little more. 'Maybe they'll never find out – perhaps the fish have eaten his face off or something.'

Even Joe couldn't take that one. 'Hell, boss, he's only bin in the bleeding river a coupla days ... I seen stiffs pulled out of the water after three weeks and they were still in canny shape, especially in cold weather like this.'

Jackie scowled. 'Fine comfort you are! So why haven't the police been round to see his employers – that's us?' He threw himself down on to the settee. 'Better get downstairs and keep an eye on what's happening. See if you can pick anything up about Geordie. And keep yer flaming mouth shut, right!'

Joe trundled off, looking sour. As he got to the door, Jackie stopped him. 'If I know these protection bastards, they'll try to stir up more trouble pretty soon. So get hold of a few heavy lads – fellers like Paddy Flynn and Bert Howard. Tell them there's a fiver a night and free booze if they hang around and be ready for a punch-up ... OK?'

Joe grinned, his good humour restored. A free fight was something that he *did* understand. He loped off, rubbing his hands, not caring about the possible life sentence that hung over him and Jackie.

Chapter Eight

Next afternoon, Alec Bolam sat in his room waiting for a call to MacDonald's room.

His sergeant waited, too. Jimmy was sprawled in his favourite position near the window, where he could look across at the office girls in the Civic Centre opposite.

There was silence as Jimmy watched the girls and Alec studied that morning's newspaper.

'*The Journal*'s done a good spread on the Bigg Market affair,' he said suddenly. 'They've never had it so good, a murder *and* a clubland feud all in the same issue.'

'Poor old Mac must be doing his nut,' cackled Grainger, irreverently. 'He was paddling about the Tyne till God knows what time, then he gets our little lot thrown at him!'

Alec nodded and folded up the paper. 'What goes on with this killing, I wonder? Had any news from your low friends in Photography?'

'Stumped, so I hear. The dredger took half his head off, so they haven't a clue who he is. Young bloke, apparently – beaten to death. No missing persons to tally with him.'

'Maybe a protection job from Bradford or Leeds – or perhaps Papagos and Casella brought him up with them from the Smoke!' said Bolam facetiously.

Neither of them knew how near to the truth they were when they jokingly coupled the murder with the clubs, but Geordie Armstrong was miles from their thoughts, especially since the previous night's trouble at the club had monopolized their attention.

'What happened to those characters, anyway?' asked Bolam.

'Left on the ten fifteen for King's Cross … quite openly.'

Alec smiled cynically. 'I'll bet they were more than open. They'd have taken bloody good care to have been noticed by as many people as possible, knowing that their boys were going to lob a bomb through Jackie's window an hour after the train left!'

'What d'you think the next move will be?' asked Jimmy Grainger.

'Jackie won't squeal to us, that's for sure. And he's too stubborn to pay up protection money without a fight, so it looks like a war, unless the Greek and his pal decide to try an easier victim.'

The sergeant rose from his window ledge and stretched. 'Are we going to keep tabs on the Bigg Market all the time now?'

Bolam frowned. 'Difficult … there's only thee and me, unless Uncle Mac decides to give us some more men on attachment. We'll have to try and keep a watch on the Rising Sun at least once a night between us.'

The phone rang to call them to MacDonald's office.

As they walked along the corridor, Alec passed on a bit more news. 'I've heard from the Interpol Office at The Yard … the Danish police have got nothing on Hansen – Jackie's manager.'

'Is it his real name?' asked Grainger.

'Yes, they've checked his antecedents. He's got no form in London, either. Was in the clubs there but, as far as we know, he's clean right through.'

They reached the superintendent's door and went in. MacDonald was looking even more haggard than usual.

'What do you want to do about these yobs from London?' he asked without any preamble. When things were pressing, Mac cut out all the frills.

'Nothing we *can* do, unless they come back for more, sir. Or if we could get someone to "cough" … Stott won't, that's for sure,' said Bolam with feeling.

'Not turned up anybody who could have thrown that bomb?'

'No, not a sniff. Anyone with a record of violence like Papagos and Casella can get mouths to shut and stay shut. The local rogues would rather do a stretch than squeal on them.'

'Any lead from the forensic lab on that bomb?'

'No, not so far. They must have brought it from London with them – chucking incendiaries isn't an old Tyneside tradition. Any progress on your big job from last night, sir?'

MacDonald began stoking his pipe with tobacco.

'As unpromising as your Rising Sun, Alec. We're afraid he might be a complete outsider, from Yorkshire or even Glasgow, perhaps. With all the ships in and out of that part of the river, he may even have been slung overboard.'

Potts cut in for the first time. 'In the three to six days that he might have been in the river, there have been thirty-one vessels on the move. Some of them on their way to the Persian Gulf and even Hong Kong now. Bloody hopeless job trying to trace them all.'

'We're in the doldrums on both jobs, then,' commented Bolam. 'I think we'll have to ask for Press and TV assistance on trying to trace any car rushing through the Bigg Market at eleven twenty last night. Some unsuspecting citizen who doesn't know that Casella might carve him up, may come forward and give us a lead.'

'What about stolen vehicles last night?' asked Mac.

'Seven altogether, not accounted for at the time of the incident,' put in Grainger. 'Four of them recovered, nothing to connect them with the Bigg Market.'

MacDonald now had his pipe going like the funnel of the

Shields' ferry. 'Who have we got on Tyneside who could pull a bomb job like this?'

Bolam shrugged. 'As I said, sir, chucking paraffin bombs isn't really the done thing in the North-East – so far, thank God. I've got a sneaky feeling that Papagos and friend may have imported somebody, car and all. In fact, how else could they have arranged a thing like that in an hour? They were in the Rising Sun until nine thirty, according to Herbert Lumley – then they left on the ten fifteen train, and the bomb was thrown at eleven twenty. They must have had the whole thing set up beforehand. When Jackie Stott gave them the bum's rush, they just lifted a finger to their boys and that was that!'

Potts nodded. 'The fire-raisers could have been over the High Level Bridge less than a minute after it went off and through Gateshead five minutes later.'

'And back in London by four this morning,' completed MacDonald. 'Just have to wait and see. Keep the routine stuff going, Alec. Might happen across some little thing.'

Just then an urgent rapping came at the door and a sergeant from the Fingerprint department almost fell inside, in his eagerness.

He waved a message form and planted it in front of the detective chief superintendent.

'Reply from NECRO, sir. I shrunk those fingertips down last night and got a fair set of prints off this morning. Sent 'em down to Aycliffe with a car – they just telexed through … they've got him, sir!'

MacDonald grabbed the flimsy and devoured it with his eyes.

'Well, I'm damned … here, Alec, be my guest!'

He poked the form across at the end of a long arm.

The chief inspector read the message almost incredulously.

'Geordie!' he whispered. 'Geordie Armstrong!'

Thor Hansen had arranged some days earlier to go down to

Middlesbrough to deal with more matters concerning the opening of the new club there.

He left Newcastle in his new Rover 2000 just before noon, taking Laura with him. They stopped for lunch at the Bridge Hotel, on the A1 just outside Durham and over coffee in the elegant dining room, the Dane allowed himself to be drawn into discussing his plans.

'I didn't expect Papagos to get so violent last night. I thought he would give Jackie a day or two to change his mind.'

Laura lit a cigarette with nervous hands. '*You* didn't expect it! I was scared rotten when that thing went off! What if I'd been standing near it – I could a' been killed or scarred for life.'

Thor slipped a hand over hers. 'I know. It was a damn fool thing to do without warning … and I'll tell Papagos when I see him today.' He sighed. 'Unfortunately, those fellows aren't people you can tell off very easily.'

She frowned at him. 'Thor, you're going to be right under their thumb if this goes through.'

He nodded. 'For a little time … but I have to accept that, it's a stepping stone to a lot of money, then we'll get out.'

Laura looked at him with curiosity. 'I'd match your brain against any ten of them, pet. You've had this thing worked out a long time, eh?'

'Ever since I came up north. I knew Papagos in Soho. Then a few months ago I ran into him again. At first he just wanted to start running protection up here, but there was nothing in that for me. So we agreed to chase Jackie out – the Greek would buy the business and put me in as manager.'

'But where's it going to end? You can't take over from the Papagos crowd; they'd kill you without thinking twice,' said Laura.

He looked calmly at her. 'I know that – but in two,

maybe three years I can milk enough from the business to clear out and go back to Copenhagen to start my own club ... a real high-class place, with you as the star attraction.'

He squeezed her hand again and pushed his chair back. 'We'd better be getting on, if I'm to see Papagos in Darlington before we go on to Middlesbrough.'

He paid the cheque and they went out to the Rover.

In Darlington, Thor dropped Laura to look around the shops for half an hour while he went for a conference with the Greek and his Sicilian knife man.

They had climbed aboard the London train quite openly on the previous evening, but had got off at the second stop forty minutes later, taking care not to advertise themselves too much. Now they were staying in the guest room of a well-respected public house in the town centre, keeping to their bedrooms until the evening, when they were due to go on a round of the clubs on Teesside with the object of selling a little more 'insurance'.

At a less salubrious lodging, three streets away, two large men with Birmingham accents were also lying low. At the back of their digs a large Ford was parked, the boot smelling strongly of paraffin. Although a good thirty-five miles from Newcastle, they felt it wise to lie very low. They respected the reputation of the Durham Constabulary as being amongst the hottest coppers in the country.

In Casella's bedroom, the two protection men held an audience with Hansen.

'How did Stott take last night's little warning?' asked Papagos with a leer.

'Nearly blew his top. I don't know the details, but I think he's got his bodyguard, Joe Blunt, to organize some sort of defence force – a few local thugs from the town.'

Casella sneered. 'Our boys will eat 'em alive. We'll be too busy tonight with these clubs down here, but tomorrow, we can let 'em loose on Stott again – he got a lesson coming for messing my knife arm around!'

The viciousness in his voice chilled even the experienced Dane.

Kostas Papagos frowned at Thor as Casella went across to pour the inevitable whiskies that always fuelled conferences like this. 'Let's get down to the real business. When are we going to slap him down with the news that this is a takeover, not just us selling protection? And what's this hot news you were on about on the phone this morning?'

Thor took his drink and sat on the edge of an armchair.
'The two things are connected – very much so. If you saw the papers this morning, you saw that your little bomb incident was almost pushed off the front page by a murder.'

Casella had a professional interest in murder – it was a thing near his heart. 'What's the tie-up?' he snapped.

'Jackie Stott did the killing – and I can prove it.'

The London crooks looked at each other with raised eyebrows. 'If that's on the level, we can put the black on him,' said Papagos. 'Are you sure about being able to prove it?'

Hansen wagged a finger in the general direction of his car. 'The proof is in the boot of my Rover down there.'

He told the story as fully as he knew it himself.

Papagos stalked up and down the room in triumph. 'We've got him over a barrel! The club is as good as ours, and at our price. What are the chances of squeezing him for a few thousand cash as well?'

Thor looked dubious. 'He's got very little – most of the capital is sunk in the business. He spends like water. Any cash goes through his fingers straight away. Spends a lot on his girl and only last month he bought a new Mercedes. I don't think you'd be able to blackmail him for much, except the transfer of the business.' He was desperately trying to stop his schemes being wrecked by the extortions of these over-greedy racketeers.

Casella looked disappointed. Though not a Mafioso himself, he had been brought up in the slums of Palermo and took every opportunity to practise extortion. 'What's the next move? We intend livening things up at this Rising Sun again tomorrow night.'

Hansen considered this. 'Best carry on – show Jackie that you really mean business. Then I'll get him to a meeting with you and you can pop the question about the takeover.'

Kostas Papagos nodded sagely. 'We got the money ready for a cash transaction. If he won't play, then let him know you'll drop him in it right up to the neck over this murder.'

Casella was quick to spot a possible complication. 'What happens if the bobbies pick him up for the killing, before we get to him? We'll be up the creek, then.'

'We've gotta get moving, that's all. Once it's signed and sealed, they can hang, draw and quarter him for all I care.'

Thor tried to reassure them. 'I think he's got a pretty good chance of getting away with it at the moment ... according to the radio, they can't identify the body ... perhaps never will, unless I turn in my proof.'

Casella chuckled evilly.

'Stott must be having a real bad day ... a murder rap hanging over him and someone about to cut the business from under his feet.'

Hansen smiled bleakly as he stood up. 'I must pick the girl up from the town. I'll ring you here the morning after next to fix a meeting with Stott. I take it you won't be at the disturbance tomorrow night?'

Papagos showed his full complement of gold teeth. 'Too damn right – we keep clear of anything illegal ... we don't pay dogs and then do the barking ourselves. Better get yourself a steel helmet, son, we've got a few real lively lads this time!'

Chapter Nine

Half an hour after the arrival of the message from
NECRO, a black Austin Westminster and a white Ford
Zephyr sped down the steep bank of Dean Street towards
Newcastle's quayside.

In the first were MacDonald, Potts and Alec Bolam, the
second CID car being filled with Jimmy Grainger and a
few lads from the crime department.

'It never entered my bloody head!' Bolam had said this
at least four times in the past thirty minutes. 'That silly
little business with Joe Blunt on Saturday night should 'a
reminded me, but of course, Geordie was seen alive and
well after it … Leadbitter's report was just of a punch-up,
not a murder.'

'What did he do to get his dabs in Records?' asked
Potts.

'False pretences in Stockton four years ago and larceny
in Middlesbrough before that.'

'Both Teeside – I thought he was a Tynesider,' mused
the superintendent.

'He was – he just did all his thieving away from home,
thank God. Came back to work for Stott about eighteen
months past,' answered Bolam.

The car crossed the north approach to the Swing Bridge
and turned into the dingy cobbled area beneath the High
Level. The driver parked outside the little red brick
mortuary, where the coroner's officer, a flabby, lugubrious
individual, waited with the key.

He let them into the whitewashed cell where the body
lay on the solitary slab beneath a piece of rubber sheet,

which the coroner's officer whipped off.

'Well, what d'you think? Will that do for Geordie Armstrong?'

MacDonald's strong voice grated near Bolam's ear and he hurried forward to look more closely at the remains.

Interest in the importance of the identification fought with his natural revulsion. He looked at the wet, straggly hair, now cleaned of Tyne mud, and tried to ignore the horror of the face.

'That's like his hair – sort of blondy-ginger, with a bit of frizz still left in it,' he agreed after a time.

'What about his height?' put in Potts.

'Hard to say, lying on a slab,' replied Alec critically.

'Table's exactly six feet long, if that's any help,' offered the paunchy coroner's officer.

Bolam eyed the slab and tried to measure up the body with his eye. 'Five foot eight, I was told … that'd be about right.'

The chief superintendent moved towards the door. 'Come on, then. We can't get away from the evidence of the prints. I just wanted someone who knew Armstrong in life to say that there was no reason why the body couldn't be his.'

Standing outside in the cold air of dusk, MacDonald held a council of war. 'I'm afraid you're in it right up to the neck now, Bolam … you know more about the Rising Sun and Jackie Stott than any of us, so you'll have to drop the rest of the club racket and help sort this one out.'

Bolam nodded – he could wish for nothing better.

'What about the telegram, sir?' he began. 'That might give us a lead.'

Jimmy Grainger cut in rather worriedly. 'I hope that silly old sod of a landlord has kept it, sir … otherwise we'll never know which Post Office it came from.'

'Get over there right away – use one of those cars,' ordered MacDonald. 'If you get it, ring the Met for assistance in trying to trace its origin.'

The detective sergeant and a constable whisked away, leaving the rest to cram into the Zephyr.

As they drove through the city, MacDonald discussed their next moves with Bolam and Potts.

'You'd better see the Press when you get back, Potts – you're rather good at that,' he added somewhat sarcastically. 'Just give 'em the identity and ask for a general appeal for any news of his movements from Saturday night. Bolam, you'd better be tackling Stott, as soon as you can.'

There was a sudden silence. 'Reckon he did it, Alec?' The change to Bolam's Christian name went with an alteration in mood.

Bolam thought a moment. 'Yes, he could have done it. Jackie's got a record for violence, and putting the boot in like this would be well up his street; Joe Blunt can be pretty tough too and he had a grudge against Geordie, by all accounts. I think it could have been either one of them.'

'Or both,' added the canny Scot. 'But proving it is going to be a different thing, eh?'

'Yes, sir. About the two hardest nuts in Newcastle to get a "voluntary" out of!'

The chief nodded. 'Think it was done at the Bigg Market or down on that gaming boat?'

Bolam shook his head. 'Not a clue … we'll have to check Geordie's movements every inch of the way. Perhaps you can get a team organized, sir; there'll be a lot of legwork on this part of the case. I'll get Grainger and a couple of DCs to start around the pubs as soon as he gets back from the West End.'

MacDonald sucked thoughtfully at his now mercifully dead pipe. 'This telegram angle is nasty – somebody with imagination thought of that. Knew that Geordie would be missed and goes to London to send a message to delay suspicion. Who would think of a thing like that?'

'Rules Joe Blunt out, I reckon,' said Bolam. 'That punchy idiot wouldn't think of it in a million years.'

'Could be Jackie?'

'Yes – even for him, that's good going. He's not daft by a long way, but I didn't think he'd be that subtle.' MacDonald grunted. 'Not so subtle now – if we find the sender, we've nailed him for murder.'

Bolam's face evidently registered his doubts, as MacDonald launched into a further explanation.

'Look, man, you went to Jackie on the Monday morning, asking around for Geordie, to see if he wanted to lay a complaint against Joe Blunt for bashing him ... so Jackie, if he killed him, would have to lay a false blanket on Geordie's vanishing act, in case you went around to his digs.'

Alec nodded. 'Granted – but why only blame Jackie on those grounds. Anyone else who had rubbed out Armstrong would be just as anxious to cover up.'

Mac snorted. 'But they hadn't been gingered up by you nosing about – I think it's Stott,' he ended, with a stubborn note to his voice that Bolam recognized only too well.

'You get along and squeeze him, eh?' went on the chief superintendent, 'Find out if he or any of his boys went to London about that time. We'll have to try and date that telegram.' Another thought crossed his mind. 'If you think Jackie's not bright enough to have thought of that dodge, what about his Danish manager ... could he be in it?'

'I don't think so, he's always been on the straight,' Alec answered patiently, as the car rolled into the Headquarters yard.

As they split up, MacDonald fired a last salvo. 'Try to figure how Papagos and company fit into this ... see if you can fit them into Geordie's troubles.'

Alec muttered a profanity under his breath and looked at his watch ... six o'clock. *Time to slip home for a meal.*

But as soon as he put his foot inside the office, the

phone rang. 'Jimmy here – I've got a hold of the note, thank God.'

'Got a date for it?'

'Handed in at Charing Cross Road Post Office at 5 p.m. on Monday. I've already phoned the Met for assistance and they're going to do their best, but they say that in a big, busy place like that one, it'll be damn nigh impossible to find the clerk that handled it, let alone get one that remembers it. The only hope is to send down a photo of the suspects and see if anyone can pick it out.'

Bolam scowled into the phone. 'Well, hang on to that paper, whatever happens,' he warned. 'It may end up as an exhibit at Northumberland Assizes!'

'What do you want me to do next?' asked the detective sergeant.

'Get back here, pick up a couple of lads and try to trace Geordie's movements after Joe hammered him off the *Mississippi* last Saturday night.'

Grainger's voice came tinnily over the wires. 'His landlord says he was here on Sunday – stayed in bed till one o'clock, then went out, never came back.'

'Good, good! Get a statement from that old feller, before he forgets or drops dead or something!'

He rang off, locked the drawers of his desk and headed for home.

Detective Superintendent Potts' press handout came too late for either the evening papers or the local television news. In spite of Jackie having his eyes glued to his screen and his reading of the *Chronicle*, he had no idea that the body had been identified when Alec Bolam came to see him just before eight o'clock.

The club was officially open, but only one or two enthusiastic drinkers were there, already soaking at the bar when Bolam walked in and left his hat on the old soldier's counter.

Herbert Lumley gave him a grave, 'Good evening.

Nasty bit of trouble last night, sir,' he offered.

Alec looked through the glass doors as he stood with the doorkeeper. 'You've done a good job of clearing up … still a bit of paraffin in the air, though.'

'Yessir … Mr Hansen, he organized new carpets, furniture – the lot!' Herbert grimaced fiercely. 'If I could lay my hands on them bastards that did it – the boss thinks that they'll be back to cause more trouble. He's got Joe Blunt to round up some toughs to try to protect the place …'

He stopped and looked apologetically at the policeman. 'Perhaps I shouldn't be telling you this, sir.'

Bolam slapped his shoulder. 'That's all right, Herbert. I guessed that Jackie wouldn't take this lying down. If I were you, I'd look around for another job – this one isn't going to last long, I'm afraid.'

With this cryptic advice, he moved through the doors to have a closer look at the aftermath of the fire, before looking for Stott.

Upstairs, Jackie was getting slightly drunk, while Thor Hansen and Laura Levine looked at him with curiosity, rather than distaste. Today he had drunk far more than usual, a thing he rarely did. Normally he kept a good grip on his cunning mind.

'Why are you hitting the bottle so much, Jackie?' snapped Laura. 'What's the idea of getting plastered? … I thought you would want to be on your toes, in case those protection fellows come busting in again.'

He glowered at her, swaying across the room to stand menacingly above her. 'I know what I'm bloody doing – if I wanna drink, I'll have it, not ask your flaming permission!'

Laura flushed and stood up. 'OK, if that's how you feel, to hell with you … I'm going back to my place.'

She looked across at Thor, the silent spectator, as usual.

'I'll be back by ten thirty, Thor, for my spot – though why I bother to help keep you in business, God knows,' she ended viciously, swinging back to Jackie.

He made a rude noise at her and she stalked out to get her coat from the hall. Thor saw her out and gave her a surreptitious kiss on the back of the neck when the open door shielded them from Jackie's eyes.

The Dane came back into the room and looked thoughtfully at his employer. Jackie was planted in the middle of the lounge, feet apart, shoulders back and chest stuck out.

'Thor, I'm in a hell of a mess – hell of a damn mess,' he muttered throatily.

The Dane murmured something non-committal. It was too soon to show his hand ... he knew well enough what was bothering Jackie and it wasn't the protection threats!

'I can't tell you, that's the hell of it – just can't tell you! ... wish I could, you'd soon sort something out, but I don't wanna drag you into it, see.'

He said this in a tone that half-hoped that the Dane would encourage him into purging his soul of the truth.

'Is it about Papagos?' asked Hansen, just fishing.

'Like hell it is,' snorted Stott, 'I can eat them alive, with one arm behind my back. No, Thor, it's something else. I'll get wrong with the coppers if it comes out. Real bad, this time.'

Hansen nodded and moved towards the door. 'I'd better get downstairs and see if everything is all right for opening time.'

Jackie called him back from the hall. 'I didn't tell you yet, but Joe Blunt will be getting in some strong-arm boys, in case those yobs show up again. They'll have a real nice welcome!'

'Won't do the custom any good, either way,' commented Hansen, 'Folk don't like getting mixed up in punch-ups and police raids any more than paraffin bombs.'

He thought he might as well lay the groundwork for Jackie's disillusionment as soon as possible.

Stott suddenly turned nasty. He hurled his empty whisky glass into the fireplace where it shattered into a hundred pieces. 'Why the hell did this have to happen just now?' he snarled. 'Everything comes all at once!'

'A good time to sell out, while you're on top,' suggested Thor warily, still trying to gauge the reaction. 'Let somebody else buy the trouble from you – there's bound to be an increase in the protection game now that it's started.'

He half expected Jackie to blow up again, but he did not. 'You might have something there … the spot I'm in, and Laura gone sour … I could do with a nice beach in South America if I had forty thousand quid to go with it.'

He kicked petulantly at a fragment of broken glass, then slumped down on to the settee.

Thor went out quickly and closed the door after him.

Downstairs, he found the now familiar figure of Detective Chief Inspector Bolam. 'Waiting for more trouble, Mr Bolam?' he asked pleasantly.

Alec smiled without humour. 'I'm waiting for my sergeant to show up. Is Jackie Stott about?'

'Mr Stott is upstairs,' replied the Dane, with the slightest of emphasis on the 'Mister'.

Alec looked around. 'You've done a good job on the clearing up – but a few chairs and a new carpet won't bring back all the frightened patrons.'

Hansen smiled. 'Memories are short – in a week or two, if there's no more trouble, it may even be an asset. Some people like to think they're living dangerously!'

Bolam looked at him hard. 'You don't think that Papagos and his boys are going to leave it at that, do you? They'll be back and I'm afraid there's nothing I can do to stop them.'

Hansen rather got on his dignity. 'I thought that's what

the police force was for.'

'Oh, come off it! ... we can't do a thing until some further offence is committed. And what does it matter to the Greek if a few of his hired thugs are nicked? He can get plenty more by flashing a few quid under their noses.'

Thor thought that he might get a little information for nothing.

'Why can't you arrest Papagos if you're so sure he's behind it?'

Bolam looked at him with curiosity. 'I've heard you're honest, but surely you're not all that naive! ... we can't touch them without evidence. They never soil their hands with rough stuff and no one will give evidence against them for fear of getting either themselves or their families carved up.'

He turned as Jimmy Grainger came bounding up the stairs from the street, his raincoat flying open and a rakish trilby perched on the front of his head. He opened his mouth to speak, but Bolam gave a warning nod in the direction of the manager.

'Mr Stott's up in the flat, you said.' He emphasized Jackie's title in his turn, with some sarcasm.

They left the Dane standing in tall and elegant silence and made their way up the carpeted stairs. At the top, Jimmy gave a quick rundown on his investigations during the past couple of hours.

'We've been around some of the pubs that Geordie used. We found that he was in the Cross Inn in Grainger Street early on Sunday evening, about seven thirty.'

'There's a lot more boozers you could have got around in that time,' said Bolam uncharitably.

'I know, we've got a lot to do yet ... we learnt a bit more, though. In the Bobby Shaftoe, we had a word with the landlord – he hadn't seen Armstrong for a week past, but he said that a feller called Archie Lee had been very thick with him recently.'

111

Alec Bolam nodded thoughtfully. 'I know Archie. I put him away for a year for "larceny by a servant" when I was in the East End. They used to call him the "Creeper" … he's got form for housebreaking as well.'

They kept their voices down, though it was unlikely that Jackie Stott would have his ears glued to the other side of his door.

'Have you picked up Archie?' asked Bolam.

'No, we only got on to this a few minutes past … I sent a man over to the East End to find out where he's living … the landlord only knew it was somewhere in Byker.'

'A good start – we'll need all the circumstantial stuff we can lay our hands on for this one. Come on, let's beard the lion in his den!'

He raised his fist and banged on the door. After the second attempt, there was some shuffling from the other side and the door was jerked partly open.

Stott's acne-scarred face glared out, his eyes unusually red-rimmed. His fiery complexion seemed to fade rapidly as he saw who his visitors were.

'Wotcha want?' he rumbled.

'We'd like to come in and ask a few questions, Jackie.' Bolam's voice was as smooth as silk.

'Thought we went over all that last night – I never heard of no Papagos nor Casella … and I don't know nor bloody care who threw that bomb, so do me a favour and be off, will yer!'

Both the detectives knew Stott well, but they had never seen him so bleary and rattled before. At that moment, Bolam became convinced in his earlier suspicion that this was Geordie's killer. He decided to hammer whilst the iron was so obviously hot.

'Nothing to do with last night … I want to know what happened to Geordie Armstrong.'

The door flew wide open and hit the wall with a crash.

Jackie stormed out. 'What the flaming hell are you on about!' he blustered. 'What the devil do I care about Armstrong? He's in London, ain't he? Could be in hell for all I care.'

Bolam remained impassive. 'He may well be, Jackie … he certainly isn't in London.'

Stott glared from one to the other as he stood blocking the doorway with his solid body.

Bolam pushed past him into the flat. 'Let's have a little talk, shall we – about poor old Geordie Armstrong.'

Jackie would have been well within his rights to have thrown them out for illegal entry, but he was too worried about the last remark.

He was confused – as far as he knew up to that point, the body from the river had not been identified. But what about that crack about Geordie being in hell?

He let them in and slammed the door.

They all stopped in the middle of the lounge, where Bolam's first words snuffed out any flicker of hope in Jackie's mind. 'We've found Geordie … stark naked in the Tyne, bound hand and foot.'

The snappy, matter-of-fact approach was calculated to see how the ex-boxer reacted. Considering his alcohol level, he rode it very well. He licked his lips a few times, but stayed silent for a full ten seconds whilst the wheels whirred inside his head. Somehow, he felt the shock less than he had feared … all along, he had secretly been resigned to the eventual identification of Geordie's body.

'I'm sorry – about Geordie I mean … but what's it got to do with me?'

The mechanical expression of regret took an upward lilt of aggression and Bolam sighed inwardly. It was obviously going to be a fight to the finish. Any hopes he had of the sudden shock jolting Stott into an admission, died for good.

'We think you did it – or you and Joe Blunt,' he said

113

almost conversationally.

Jackie was now himself again and if the shock hadn't rocked him into a confession, it had certainly sobered him up. His cunning mind was now working as well as usual.

'You can't damn well say that to me,' he roared with false indignation. 'I'll have you for libel.'

'Slander,' said Jimmy Grainger automatically. Bolam scowled at him, then back at Jackie.

'I can say it and I will … you and Joe were mixed up in that affair of thumping Geordie Armstrong on Saturday night. And he died on the Sunday.'

Alec turned the supposition into fact for his own purposes.

'So what? … a kick in the pants is a hell of a long way from murder.' The clubman buttoned his collar and pushed his tie up as if preparing for battle.

'You had a violent quarrel … Armstrong vanished and a false telegram was sent to his lodging to allay suspicion. I think you sent that telegram, Stott – or you had it sent.'

From that moment, the familiar 'Jackie' became 'Stott' when Bolam addressed him – it marked a significant change in the detective's attitude to his suspect.

Jackie had his feelings well under control now. He sneered the next words. 'I don't know a thing, copper!'

'I want to know your movements on Sunday – all of them.'

'Get stuffed!'

Bolam sighed again. It was going to be even harder than he thought. 'I'll have to take you to Headquarters for questioning, then.'

The ex-boxer gave a derisory laugh. 'Ha-bloody-ha! … you won't, chum! I've been in and out of too many courts in my time, not to know my rights. If you're not going to charge me, I'm staying right here and keeping my trap shut – see?'

Bolam began to get angry. If everyone knew 'their rights' as well as Stott, the police would never get a conviction. Once more he cursed the politicians who fell over backwards to make laws that favoured the villains and obstructed the police.

'Well, let's have a bit of sense and answer them here.'

'I'm not saying another bleeding word without my solicitor – except to say "get out"!' roared Jackie.

'None of this is going to help you in the long run, Stott,' snapped Bolam, 'And I'm well within my rights in staying on club premises so long as you hold a licence from the magistrates.'

'This flat isn't club premises – it's my home. Now I'm telling you to clear out of it, see.' Jackie strode over to the door and yanked it open. 'Get lost, coppers,' he snarled.

The detectives reluctantly moved towards the door. 'You'd better get that solicitor around here by the morning, Stott,' warned Bolam, as he went out. 'You're only making a rod to beat your own back, acting like this.'

Jackie spat a foul word at them and slammed the door.

'Bastard!' said Grainger feelingly.

'He knows the form a damned sight too well,' grumbled Alec, starting down the stairs. 'Let's go and see Joe Blunt … though I'll bet Jackie is on the blower to him this very minute.'

He was right. The second the door slammed behind them, Stott had dialled the number of the *Mississippi* and told his henchman what had happened.

'I know,' came Joe's voice. 'There's a rozzer here with me now.'

The club proprietor cursed into the instrument.

Jimmy Grainger, showing the astuteness that would one day make him a superintendent, had sent one of his detective constables down to the gaming boat with orders to stay there until Bolam arrived.

Joe Blunt was not in the same class as Stott when it came to defending his legal rights and had stood blinking at the policeman when he had announced that he was going to stay in the office on the boat, all night if needs be. In fact, as Blunt spoke on the phone, the DC was recording every word into his notebook.

That was until Jackie's voice exploded down the phone into Joe's ear. 'Get him outta there, you stupid git! … divvent say a thing to him, heave him off the boat and keep any others off – d'yer understand me?'

The line went dead with a thunderous click and Joe was left standing in a haze of bewilderment.

'You gotta clear off,' he said uncertainly to the detective. 'You got no right without a warrant or something.'

He shunted the officer out, against protests. Like Bolam, he knew that he'd no legal right to question Joe if he cared to object – the usual bluff wouldn't work against people who knew the law.

At the gangway, he stalled and tried to bamboozle Joe into making a statement, but the piggy-faced bruiser had Stott's instructions firmly fixed in his mind and he could not be budged from his obstinate silence.

Just as the detective was giving up in disgust, a white police Zephyr drew up on the quayside and Bolam and Grainger stepped out.

Joe stood guard on the gangway like Horatio holding the bridge. 'You're not to come aboard.' Jackie had told him not to say who had given him these orders, so he just kept repeating them like a ritual chant.

Bolam marched straight up to him and looked him hard in the eye. 'Cut it out, Joe … I know your boss told you to try it on, but it won't work. As a police officer, I have access to this boat as long as it isn't a private club – which it isn't. So get out of the blasted way, will you?'

Joe was in a quandary but he stood his ground.

Alec Bolam began to lose his patience. 'If you want it the hard way, Joe … for the last time, are we coming aboard or not?'

Joe bared his teeth in a grimace of indecision. 'No!' he grated.

Bolam beckoned up his sergeant and detective constable. 'Right … I'm arresting you for obstructing a police officer in the course of his duty – visiting licensed premises. Get in the car.'

Joe was almost in tears over his dilemma.

Jimmy Grainger put a hand on his arm. 'In the car, Joe,' he said firmly.

The ex-pug shook the hand off angrily. The other officers closed in. 'Don't start anything, Joe,' pleaded Bolam. 'We'll all get hurt for nothing. Just come quietly.'

As a reply, Joe Blunt gave Grainger a push in the chest that sent him skidding backwards for about six feet. He just managed to keep his balance, then came back to join the other two as they grappled with the defender.

Bolam and the DC grabbed an arm each and attempted to immobilize Joe, but he flung the constable off and rammed Bolam against the rail with a thump that knocked most of the breath from the chief inspector. Grainger seized the free arm and the makings of a real fight were getting under way when a white Mercedes streaked across the cobbles, banged over the railway lines and squealed to a stop at the foot of the gangway.

Jackie Stott shot out of the driving seat and yelled at the top of his voice, 'Joe … for God's sake, lay off trying to fight the whole damn police force, will yer!'

Instantly, the big thug went limp in Bolam's grip. They all turned to watch the club owner striding towards them. 'What's going on – more police victimization?'

'As if you didn't know,' panted Bolam. 'This man of yours physically tried to prevent us entering these premises. I've arrested him and I'm taking him back to the

Central Police Station.'

'You bloody fool, Joe ... you always seem to be scrapping on this flaming gangway.' He glowered at the policemen. 'Are you trying to bust into my boat as an inspector of clubs or as a murder investigator?'

'Stop trying to buck the truth, Stott,' Bolam snapped. 'Joe here has committed an offence. Other charges – more serious ones – may be held against him later. He's going into the cells for the night.'

Jackie pushed past them angrily. 'OK, OK, take him! I'm going to ring for my solicitor to be there ... so Joe, divvent open your flaming mouth until he arrives, d'yer hear ... wait for Lupin to show up before you even give these bums the time of day.'

He marched to the door, leading down to the bowels of the *Mississippi*.

Bolam called after him, 'I'll be back at the Bigg Market in the morning, Stott. I'll want some statements, so you'd better have your solicitor there then.'

'*And* I'll have a search warrant for this old tub, too,' he added under his breath.

Chapter Ten

Joe Blunt probably owed his life to Alec Bolam, though the detective got no thanks for it. While the punch-drunk caretaker of the *Mississippi* languished in a bare cell at Newcastle's Central Police Station, two of Papagos' thugs broke into the deserted boat with axes and hacked a two-foot hole below the waterline. The old vessel gently subsided on to the mud and at high tide her gaming room and office were filled to the deck head with black Tyne water.

If Joe had been in his bed, he would probably have been knocked unconscious and left to drown, as the Midland mobsters who did the job had not the faintest idea of tides or water depths.

Papagos knew what he was doing when he ordered this particular bit of vandalism, which he had kept from Thor Hansen. Hansen's news about his 'dead cert' opportunity of blackmailing Jackie had decided him on this extra outrage. He was not particularly interested in taking over a third-rate gambling joint on the river. By sinking it, he aimed to kill two birds with the one stone – as a potent demonstration to Stott that he really meant business and to add a fair dollop of insurance money to the assets of the Stott empire, which he aimed to take over within a day or two.

Next morning, Stott was almost apoplectic with rage when the River Police rang him at seven thirty to tell him that his boat was squatting on the bottom with dirty water sloshing from every crack. After going down to the quayside to view the wreck, he tore back to the Bigg

Market in a blind fury and rang his solicitor. Within the hour the lawyer was sitting in the lounge. He declined the whisky which Jackie seemed to be using instead of breakfast.

'You've got three problems all together here, Mr Stott,' said Lupin, the lawyer, after Jackie had vitriolically outlined recent events. 'One, you'll need to go ahead with an insurance claim on the boat. Two, you need a bail application for Joe Blunt. Three, you need to make a statement over this nonsense about the murder of Armstrong.'

Abel Lupin was under no illusions about his client. Indeed, his law practice was such that he had few illusions about most of his customers.

A rare combination of Ulsterman and Hebrew, Lupin had a flourishing and lucrative practice as a criminal lawyer in the North-East. Not for him the mundane work of conveyancing or probate, unless it be the leasehold of a strip joint or the fiddling of *inter vivos* gifts of some elderly survivor of the '45 black market. His main work was the defence of professional criminals, great and small, though he did a fair trade in any legal proceedings which had the police as its target. The merest whisper of an illegal arrest or malicious prosecution and Abel was there like a flash. Let a copper put a foot over your threshold without a warrant and Lupin was your man! All club owners, though they might hate each other like poison, had one thing in common – they all had Abel Lupin as their 'legal eagle'.

He sat in one of Jackie's armchairs now, his body flowing over the sides. He was not a big man – he was enormous! His eighteen stone looked like a half-melted wax model, dressed in a black jacket and grey striped trousers.

He was careful not to ask Jackie whether he had in fact killed Geordie Armstrong. If he had said 'yes', even

Lupin's elastic ethics would have been a little overstretched. Instead, he carried on with the tacit assumption that his job was to steer Stott clear of as much trouble as possible.

'They're bringing Joe up before the beaks this morning,' growled Jackie. 'Obstructing the police or some such bullshine.'

Abel nodded sagely. 'If he laid a hand on them, he'll be remanded until he's committed to the next Quarter Sessions. Sounds like a nasty, vindictive charge because they couldn't bluff their way aboard ... we'll get bail all right on those grounds, Joe will be back here by lunchtime. Sounds as if you might need a strong right arm for tonight, if Papagos keeps up the pressure. Those London men can survive a lot of fighting, you know. They've got nothing to lose but a little time, but you've got the whole of your business to forfeit ... by the time you've given up scrapping with them, you'll find that you've lost all your custom.'

Jackie glowered at him. 'If we let the swine get away with it, they'll overrun the whole North-East.'

Abel looked at him with one of his chiding, sidelong smiles. 'Are you going to be the martyr – or sucker – for all your old rivals like Eddie Freeman? All you'll prove is that you were the first to get cut down to size.'

Stott's temper began to smoulder. 'What's the game? Have they bought you up as well?'

Abel looked offended. 'They have not! I'm trying to make you see sense. If you can't beat 'em, join 'em.'

'Pay their bloody protection! ... I'll see them dead first.'

'The boot may be on the other foot, old fellow ... no, I thought you might think of selling out. Let someone else carry the can, if there's going to be trouble. Make a payment or two to quieten things down, then flog the whole business – you're on the top of the wave now, you can only go down from here, as things are.'

'What d'yer mean – "down"?' snapped Jackie.

'Rising prices, unemployment … luxuries like strippers and gaming go to the wall first. You could clean up a nice price as it stands.'

Jackie said nothing, his anger evaporating. Thor had advised the same thing and he had a great respect for the Dane's opinion – as much as he had for the lawyer's. Now both of them said the same thing, but nevertheless, his pride overruled the idea. 'Nobody's going to push me out until I want to go, see!'

Abel Lupin grimaced a smile once more. 'But maybe you should want to go now?'

The cross talk went on for some time, leaving Jackie unconvinced but somewhat shaken in his determination to fight Papagos to the finish. Lupin eventually left, with a promise to be at the Central Police Station at ten, before Joe Blunt was due to face the justices in the adjacent Magistrates' Court. He saw Joe when the time came and firmly told him to keep his mouth clamped shut.

The preliminary remand proceedings only took a few minutes, with Lupin giving a masterly performance which made the police sound a lot of malicious, scheming rogues intent on persecuting baby-faced innocents like Joe Blunt. This resulted in the magistrates releasing him on Jackie's surety of two hundred pounds. Outside the court, Abel buttonholed Alec Bolam.

'Mr Stott is ready to make a statement about that matter you raised yesterday,' he said. 'Where and when do you want to take it?'

Alec looked at his watch. 'I've got to be at the coroner's court at ten thirty, but that'll only take a few minutes – I'll see you in my office at Headquarters at eleven.'

Lupin agreed and, as he walked back towards Stott, Bolam called after him. 'I should tell you that I've got search warrants for both the Rising Sun and the *Mississippi*,' he added ruefully, having been told only minutes before that any evidence that might have been on the boat was now swilling around below the surface of the Tyne.

Lupin, who had already gathered from Jackie that there was nothing to be feared from any search of his premises, agreed condescendingly and vanished with his client, who had kept sullenly in the background during these exchanges.

Bolam went down to the Coroner's Court, where the senior Coroner's Officer was dealing with the case of Geordie Armstrong.

Bolam arrived just as the Coroner, a nervous young man new to the office, was taking his seat at the top table in the bare upper room. Only two other witnesses were present, but there was an assortment of press reporters there, and the Coroner, a thin bespectacled figure, nervously rustled papers about whilst his officer swore in a desiccated-looking man of about fifty.

Bolam, seated at the back of the court, could hardly hear a word the man said, but he managed to gather that this was Geordie's father. His evidence was entirely negative. His son had not set foot across the family threshold in Jarrow for three years, having been 'a right disappointment' as he had done time in prison.

Dr Ellison puffed up the stairs at the last moment, in time to gabble the oath and tell the coroner that the cause of death was multiple injuries including a broken neck and fractured ribs. The deceased had been dead between three days and a week.

The reporters wrote frenziedly at this, but this was all they were going to get from the doctor, who scribbled his signature on the deposition and vanished as quickly as he had come.

Bolam was the only other witness. He took the oath in a

hard, even voice.

'You are Alec Heath Bolam, Detective Chief Inspector in the Tyneside Constabulary?'

'I am, sir.'

'And you can identify the body as that of George William Armstrong?'

'Not directly, sir, though I knew him during life and the body shows no features inconsistent with that identity, though it has suffered severe post-mortem injuries. However, I am in possession of a report from the North-East Criminal Records Office which establishes beyond doubt that the deceased was in fact George Armstrong.'

Bolam handed over the flimsy message form for the coroner to study.

He handed it back. 'Er – that seems good enough. I understand that certain investigations are taking place?'

'Yes, sir – no one has yet been charged.'

There was a slight emphasis on the 'yet' which sent the reporters' pens skidding across their notebooks.

'In that case, I shall adjourn the inquest for six weeks under Section Twenty of the Coroner's Amendment Act. If I hear from another court that proceedings are being taken, this enquiry will, of course, not be resumed.'

The business was over and a few minutes later Alec Bolam was back in Headquarters. In the afternoon, MacDonald called another conference.

'Are we sure we've got nothing to pull Stott down with?' he began. His wrinkled, long face radiated annoyance over the group of detectives.

Bolam rocked his head slowly from side to side. 'Not a thing – that statement he made this morning was a complete farce. Denied setting eyes on Geordie after the Saturday night – denied sending any telegram – in fact it was a waste of ten minutes, that interview – Abel Lupin put Jackie up to it – sat there and blocked half my questions, damn him!'

MacDonald scowled. 'And no hope of a voluntary statement from Joe Blunt, either?'

Bolam shook his head. 'Lupin's told him to keep his face shut too. If we could prove even one of our suspicions, it would be a start, but at present the DPP[2] would laugh at us if we sent him a file on it – and Lupin would jump on us for malicious prosecution and unlawful arrest.'

MacDonald nodded wearily. 'I know, you're right. But we know the bugger did it – how are we going to nail him!'

Potts, the expert police lawyer, chipped in. 'What about the lab? With all this circumstantial stuff, we need some real physical evidence from somewhere if we're to get this one off the ground.'

Alec grimaced. 'We've been over the Rising Sun with a toothcomb today – not a thing. Jackie was grinning all over his mug – he knows there's nothing there to find.'

'And the *Mississippi* is under the bloody river,' moaned MacDonald. 'No chance *they* did it to destroy any evidence, I suppose?'

Bolam threw up his hands. 'God knows … I doubt it; Jackie's the wrong sort to destroy his own property. In spite of being a fly bastard, he's got a streak of arrogance that might pay off for us in the end – thinks he's God's right-hand man. I can't see him scuttling his own boat.'

'Papagos and company are behind that, no doubt,' observed Potts. 'So that line's dead – we'll never get a smell of whoever did it. But what about Armstrong's movements that Sunday night?' he demanded.

Jimmy Grainger spoke up. 'We traced him finally to the Berwick Arms on the Quayside. He was in the bar there about ten o'clock – no one saw him after that.'

'The Berwick … not far from the boat,' mused

---

[2]Director of Public Prosecutions

125

MacDonald.

'But useless as evidence,' reminded Bolam. 'We can't tie in Jackie or Joe Blunt with the boat that night.'

'Where do they say they were?' demanded the Chief Superintendent.

'They don't – not a word from either of 'em since Lupin shut them up,' snapped Bolam.

MacDonald scratched his thin grey hair.

'Where do we go from here?'

There was a heavy silence for a moment.

'What about that telegram?' he asked again.

Jimmy spoke up once more. 'No luck, sir. The Met chaps showed pictures of Joe and Jackie from Records to the Post Office staff, but no one recognized them. Not surprising, I suppose.'

'So that line is dead,' grunted the detective chief.

Alec cleared his throat. 'We had a word or two with the "Creeper" – this Archie Lee that Geordie was hanging around with. He was as scared as hell – I couldn't gather who he was frightened of; it wasn't us, though.'

'I thought he'd vanished,' said Potts.

'He did – as far as Blaydon … went to ground in his sister's place.

'Get anything out of him?' asked MacDonald.

'Only that he and Geordie were working some little fiddle at Jackie's expense. He was playing the tables with Armstrong as croupier, and Armstrong slipped him a few extra chips or moved him on to a winning square when nobody was looking.'

'So that's why Jackie gave him the push!' summarized MacDonald.

'And probably why Joe was giving him a belting on Saturday night – but I can't see him getting killed for it,' objected Bolam.

The chief superintendent pursed his lips. 'Never can tell. Though it does seem a bit drastic. And why belt him on Saturday and then wait until Sunday to kill him?'

There was another heavy silence.

'And the lab have turned up nothing?' persisted Potts.

Bolam took a deep breath. 'Very little. There was a small amount of alcohol in the body, no more than from a steady night's boozing. The wire around the legs was a common type of galvanized fencing wire. Made in Britain, according to the lab people. They're comparing it with a few samples from different manufacturers, but they need a lot more time before they could have a chance to pin it down to one factory. Even if they do, there's a hell of a lot of fencing wire used all over the North, so I don't see that bringing it much nearer Jackie Stott.'

'The dredger didn't fetch up anything more?' asked MacDonald.

'No – they scratched around for half a day, but no joy.' This time it was Potts doing the answering. 'I asked about the possibility of using police frogmen, but they say there's ten feet of mud on the bottom, it would be a waste of time.'

MacDonald succumbed to temptation and hauled his old pipe from his pocket.

'Nothing in Jackie's place or in the back of his car?'

'Not a speck of anything to help us – the car looked too clean to be true, but that's neither here nor there.'

'Any tie-up with this other business – Papagos and crew – I wonder?'

Bolam sighed. 'God knows, sir ... I can't see how. Geordie was dead long before the Greek turned up in Newcastle.'

After a few more minutes of fruitless talk, they broke up. MacDonald had agreed to allot more men to the routine drag of asking around all the public houses and places on the Quayside, to see if they could pin Geordie's movements down more accurately. They were also very interested in the whereabouts of the two men from the

Rising Sun on that Sunday night and the enquiries 'on the knocker' were designed to try to get a lead on that aspect as well. All motor patrols were to be questioned in case Stott's conspicuous Mercedes had been seen anywhere that night – in fact, all the tedious routine of a murder investigation began to roll.

Back in his office, Bolam kicked his waste-paper basket in disgust. 'Looks as if Jackie will be able to sit back and laugh at us, blast him,' he snarled.

'He won't have much time for sitting back, with the Greek on his tail,' countered Jimmy. 'Which fox are we going to chase – Jackie or the Papagos mob?'

Bolam settled for the latter – the killing seemed to be stagnant until they got some sort of break.

'We'll stake out the Rising Sun for a few hours tonight – sit outside in a car ... that old Austin won't be noticed at one of the meters in the Bigg Market.'

'All night?' queried Jimmy in dismay.

'From about eleven till two – that's the peak customer time. If the London yobs are going to try anything on, it'll be in that period.'

'And if nothing happens?'

'We try again tomorrow – and the next night. Get one of the younger lads from downstairs – a newish fellow, that won't be recognized in the club. Tell him to go in and wait – give us the tip if anything starts.'

Jimmy looked unsettled. 'What about the murder angle? Are we just going to let it ride?'

Bolam shrugged. 'Uncle Mac is running that – he'll have you on the pub routine unless you stick to my bandwagon, chum! Wearing out their boots on doorsteps seems to be the menu for most of the CID for the next week. Never know, something might come of it, too ... hard graft usually brings in more rewards than flashes of inspiration in this game.'

With this Jimmy had to be satisfied and they parted until the late evening.

Bolam left the house in his usual sullen rage at about eight thirty, after stonily refusing to be drawn by taunts about yet another night spent in club-crawling.

His daughter had gone upstairs soon after tea and kept out of the way until she heard the front door slam and the Morris reverse noisily from the drive. Then she came down and joined her mother in a cup of tea in the kitchen.

'I'll bet he's gone there again tonight – he knows I always go to see Freddie on a Saturday,' she said almost tearfully.

Vera Bolam felt torn between sympathy for her daughter and an almost reflex need to make excuses for Alec as soon as he was out of earshot.

'I know, pet, but he *is* mixed up with that murder ... I gather that this man Stott is suspected of killing the Armstrong fellow.'

Betty stared stubbornly into her cup. 'I don't care!' she murmured. 'I only know that I want to see Freddie as usual.'

Vera fiddled with her spoon. She felt awkward – her previous backing of Betty's infatuation was mainly a weapon to use against Alec. But now things had gone a bit too far. This was no ordinary 'boy meets girl' affair – Betty's attitude was almost pathological; she ate, slept and lived Freddie. Three times a week, the girl went to the club, just to look at him and sit at a table for a few minutes of his company.

'Why do you always have to go on your own, Betty?' she began gently. 'After all, it's almost entirely a man's club – gambling and striptease and that ... couldn't you at least go with a friend from the office?'

Betty looked up suspiciously. *Now she's changing her tune, is she*, the girl thought. 'Did you ever go courting and take a girlfriend along, Mum?' she asked coldly and went back to staring glassily into her teacup.

Vera Bolam hardened her voice. 'Well, I don't know that it's all right, Betty. Not now that there's been all this trouble at the club. It's not safe for you to go there, really, Betty. Your father flatly forbade you to go; he said there was sure to be more trouble in the next day or two.'

Betty raised her head again and snapped at her mother. 'That's right – you start siding with him, now that it suits you! I'm mad about Freddie, I tell you … I don't care if all the gangsters in the world come there – I'm going to see him!' She jumped up and grabbed her handbag from the table. 'I'm over twenty-one now, I can do what I like. If you try to stop me, well … I'll leave home. I'm fed up here, anyway, with you and Dad always fighting.'

With this parting jibe, she ran sobbing from the room. Her feet pounded on the stairs and there was the slamming of a bedroom door.

Vera started after her, then stopped and walked slowly back to the kitchen. She felt alone, deserted.

This had been on the boil for a long time, she told herself. *Alec was right, blast him*. This Freddie, whom she had seen only once at the party, was a worthless lout, but after defending him for so long against her husband, she was having a job to climb down.

She sat down at the table and cried – not from real misery but from frustration at having a happy, pleasant life handed to her on a plate, yet knowing full well that she would not enjoy taking it.

A few minutes later, Betty came back down the stairs and the front door slammed with almost prophetic finality.

The young detective constable planted in the Rising Sun had not long to wait for trouble to start. He settled himself at the bar and kept a sharp lookout from behind a glass of McEwen's' Export Ale. Then he began chatting up the barmaid, Freda, while keeping his eyes skinned for any characters who might be infiltrating on behalf of Papagos and Casella.

There were three or four tough-looking men distributed around the room at the moment and he felt uneasy about them until Freda put him wise.

'Like our Defence Corps, love?' she chirped, hanging her prominent and over-exposed bust across the bar. He raised his eyebrows enquiringly and she jerked a thumb in the direction of the big men. 'Some of Joe Blunt's pals – recruited as Jackie's bodyguard until this protection scare is over. Glad they're there, really – I had half a mind to jack it in when that bloody bomb came in ... but we gotta stick by old Jackie in a bad patch like this ... though some I could name don't seem to care.'

She sniffed and looked pointedly across to where Laura Levine sat at a table with Thor Hansen.

The detective took the opportunity to pick up some local gossip. 'She's Jackie's girlfriend, isn't she?'

'Was, you mean ... if "girlfriend" is the right word. Every day of thirty, she is ... and *girlfriend* means jumping around a bed with him to get top of the bill at a few clubs. The other feller's her latest heart-throb.' She nodded across at the Dane. 'They been playing it real quiet until now. That damn fool Jackie can't see further than his nose, but this last day or two, they been canoodling as bold as brass. If he catches them at it, there'll be some fur flying – as jealous as hell over her, is Jackie!'

The constable filed away this bit of knowledge for Bolam, but his main interest was the gang war and about twenty minutes later, things began to happen.

On that Saturday night, in spite of the previous disturbances earlier in the week, there was an almost full house. Jackie and his manager had noticed this an hour before with some gratification, putting it at least partly down to curiosity, and the lack of any trouble on the

131

previous night.

Jackie was upstairs at the moment, keeping an eye on the gaming tables, which were also attracting a record house.

'Have to have a bomb-throwing every week, eh, Thor!' he said almost gaily to Hansen.

The fiasco of the police investigation into Geordie's death had restored his spirits, especially as he had had a favourable forecast from the insurers of the *Mississippi*.

Downstairs, the stripper was just starting her routine. Encouraged by the big audience, she was sweating herself into even more enthusiastic contortions than usual, as she swayed and squirmed amongst the tables nearest the stage.

The crowd was thick around her, most of the men standing up for a better view. The lights were out except for the brilliant spot that was focused on the dancer and the detective constable lost sight of the men who were supposed to be Jackie's private army.

The band was thumping out the rhythmic beat with which the girl's generous hips moved synchronously, punctuated by whistles and lewd remarks from the front row.

Sudden the erotic atmosphere was ruined by a piercing shriek. The stripper stopped dead and yelled the most obscene series of words the policeman had ever heard.

The band croaked to a wheezing halt as the girl swung a tremendous slap against the face of a man sitting at the edge of the dance floor.

In the sudden silence, she swore again. 'You lousy swine, I'll teach you to stub your fags out on my backside!' and she hit him again, then ran back to the platform and vanished through a door at the side.

The man she had slapped guffawed and threw a beer bottle after her. It went wide of the door and smashed against the wall above Freddie's head. He screamed with fright and there was an echoed scream from Betty Bolam, sitting alone in a corner.

The man with the roving cigarette whistled shrilly and threw another bottle, which crashed through the skin of the band's big drum, making a tearing boom.

Instantly, all hell was let loose.

The lights were still down and Thor Hansen, who was standing near the switches, made no move to snap them on.

Four or five men, who had been sitting quietly in various parts of the room, suddenly upturned their tables, began yelling and screaming and followed their leader in throwing empty bottles at the stage and lashing out indiscriminately at their neighbours in the gloom.

The terrified musicians ducked and staggered away, the organist getting a cut head in the process.

The audience degenerated into a yelling, screaming, swearing mass and Jackie's paid protectors were paralyzed by the darkness and the lack of anyone to fight.

Within seconds, there was complete pandemonium. The young detective had had his orders – no joining in, just get out and raise the alarm. Sprinting to the doors he headed off the first would-be escapers and clattered down the stairs. A few yards down the road, at the top of the Cloth Market, stood a blue Austin, with no outward signs of a police car about it. As he ran up to it, Jimmy Grainger was already getting out.

'It's started, bottle-chucking and all – hell of a shemozzle!'

Bolam grabbed the radio handset. 'Q-Four to L-K ... hello, L-K, expected disturbance at Rising Sun Club. Please send the cars as arranged. Q-Four out.'

He dropped the microphone and ran with the other officers towards the bright neon sign at the entrance to the club. Already a thin stream of dishevelled customers was straggling out, and the policemen forced their way upstairs and entered the chaos of the big room. Jackie Stott was just in front of them, having thundered down from the casino above.

'Somebody put the bloody lights on!' he yelled.

Ahead of him was the even larger figure of Joe Blunt, flailing his way through the crowd with complete disregard for friend or foe.

Herbert Lumley was standing helplessly near his cubby hole as customers besieged him for their clothes. He wanted to join in, but the frightened and angry patrons were determined to get their coats and clear off.

'Where are the switches, Herbert?' snapped Bolam, before plunging into the melee.

'On the left-hand wall, halfway to the stage.'

He hesitated.

'Mr Hansen was sitting near them. I don't know why he hasn't put them on. I hope he isn't hurt.'

Alec thrust forward against the stream of people, but before he got to the switches, the lights suddenly went up. Jackie Stott had reached them first and was now looking around wildly for someone to punch. But there was now no sign of anyone actually fighting or causing damage – the only scrap going on was between two of Jackie's own thugs who had failed to recognize each other in the darkness.

'Where are they, Joe?' yelled Jackie. 'Who done it? I'll murder 'em.'

In the heat of the moment, he forgot that his words were rather too topical to shout in the presence of policemen.

Four uniformed officers appeared at the top of the stairs and began holding back those who were trying to leave but the confusion took a long time to die down, many customers still thinking they were in mortal danger of being knifed by the Mafia.

Jimmy Grainger, who knew that Betty Bolam was supposed to be in the Rising Sun that night, forced his way towards the band platform, but failed to see any sign of her.

He did find Freddie, however. Pale and trembling, the guitarist was carrying a black handbag and trying to get back to the stage.

'Where's Betty Bolam, Freddie?' snapped Jimmy.

'I dunno, she just went out.'

'You've got her bag.'

'She left it – I'm keeping it for her.'

Jimmy was about to call him a liar, when Bolam's bull-like voice bellowed from across the room for him. Torn between getting the truth out of Freddie and the urgency in his boss's voice, Jimmy hesitated, then rammed his way back towards the chief inspector.

'Get all the exits closed and organize the uniformed men into checking all the customers and their membership cards,' he snapped, 'We've lost a canny few already, but some of them should be Papagos's boys.'

Jimmy started to talk to him about Betty, but Bolam ploughed off again to intercept Jackie Stott.

'You were bloody quick on the scene,' raved the club owner.

'Just as well – your defence team were a right flop … who kept those lights dowsed – it was tailor-made for those hoodlums to raise hell and get away with it?'

Stott swung round on Thor Hansen. 'I thought you would have seen to that … what happened?'

'I was over on the other side from the switches – I couldn't get through,' he lied easily.

Bolam swung away and found his sergeant still hovering behind him. 'Get with it, Jimmy – any sign of my daughter, by the way?'

'I've got a feeling that she went out the back way with Freddie Robson – I saw him with a handbag that could have been hers. I was going to follow, but you called.'

Bolam slapped his arm. 'You're a good lad, Jimmy. I

expect she's run off home. About time she learnt a lesson, silly bitch. Come on, let's try to nobble some of these yobs.'

After two hours' work, they managed to get enough information to arrest one man. The one, in fact, who had jabbed his cigarette at the stripper's bottom. Two nearby patrons were willing to swear that he was the one who had started the trouble. The other vandals were unidentifiable, either because they had got out before the police arrived or because no one could pinpoint them in the darkness and confusion.

The one arrested would give nothing away except his name and address ... he was from Doncaster. He had no membership card and refused to say anything at all, by far the best policy when accused of a crime. He seemed not unduly worried – he had been well paid by Papagos's henchman and had nothing to lose apart from a few weeks in prison, at the worst. He did not even know that he was working for the Greek, so could not incriminate him in any way. The thugs were no less presentable than most of the other patrons and in fact were much less repulsive than Jackie's bodyguard, so with genuine membership cards provided by Thor Hansen, there was no way of spotting them.

Stott fumed impotently up and down, looking at the wreckage. Tables were overturned, chairs broken and the walls running with beer dregs and scarred by broken glass.

'You're about finished now, Stott,' said Bolam grimly. 'Your place has been busted up twice in a few days, your customers scared half to death!'

'They'll come back – they came tonight, even after the bombing, didn't they?' Stott snarled at the detective.

'Come back! ... not the same ones, Stott. No one wants a fist up their nose or a broken bottle in their belly ... not twice! But apart from that, your licence is in danger. The police have got something better to do than keep sorting

136

out your troubles. When your licence comes up for renewal, the justices will kick you out … if the Chief Constable doesn't recommend it right away!'

Jackie went almost purple. 'This suits you right down to the bloody ground, doesn't it, Bolam!' he raved. 'You've been waiting for a chance to get the drop on me … just because you can't hang a murder on me, you're out to fix me any way you can … that and your blasted daughter!'

Bolam ruffled up like an angry cockerel. 'What the hell do you mean?'

Jackie sneered. 'D'yer think I don't know what goes on! … your kid and Freddie Robson. He's a great boy for the chicks is Freddie. He'll eat your kiddie alive, will Freddie!'

Bolam, enraged now, brought back his arm to hit Stott, but Jimmy Grainger grabbed it and levered it down.

'Don't let him rile you, sir … he's trying to drop you right in it.'

The rage passed as quickly as it had come and within seconds Alec blessed Jimmy for his intervention. Striking Stott would have cost him his job in the police force.

'You've had it, Stott … you're finished!' he gritted through his teeth.

The ex-boxer laughed triumphantly, the petty success with Bolam blinding him momentarily to all his other troubles. 'Hope you find your daughter, Bolam … Reckon I could tell you where she'll be, but I don't know Freddie's address, any more than I knew Geordie's!'

Alec ignored this final jibe and walked back to the stairs to join the rest of the policemen.

'Betty'll have been home a while by now,' reassured Jimmy, in a low voice.

But when Alec arrived home at two thirty, he was met by Vera at the front door. She was too worried to nag him, so he knew that something was seriously wrong.

'Betty hasn't come home – and she's taken a case and some of her things with her.'

Without a word, Alec squeezed her arm and pushed her inside the house.

He went back to the garage and within a minute was racing through the cold, deserted streets back to Headquarters.

Chapter Eleven

Thor Hansen managed to park his Rover within a hundred yards of the Rising Sun, and went straight up to Jackie's flat, ignoring the shambles in the first floor room, the legacy of the previous night.

Stott was drinking coffee in the lounge, bleary-eyed and unshaven and wearing a shabby dressing gown.

Thor went straight to business. 'I've just had a phone call from Kostas Papagos,' he lied. 'He's in Darlington with Casella and wants to talk business with you.'

Jackie's coarsely handsome face scowled at him. 'Why the hell didn't they ring me, then – I'm on the phone, you know!'

A day or two ago, he would never have queried Thor in this way, but the business of the lights failing to go up last night, the infiltration of the protection racketeers and the gravitation of Laura to the Dane's company was at last beginning to add up in his mind.

Thor ignored this sarcasm. 'They've changed their minds – they're not interested in selling you "insurance" any more.'

Stott's face began to light up, then it hardened. 'Something worse, eh? They got a bloody hope!'

'They say they want to buy you out – this club, the Middlesbrough option and be assigned insurance rights on the *Mississippi*. They'll give you a very fair price.'

Jackie spat out a string of very rude words and finished by glowering suspiciously at his manager. 'And where exactly do you fit into all this? I thought you were on my side, but now I'm wondering just what the hell you've been up to ... how come you're so thick with these London bums?'

Thor shrugged. He was committed to the opposition now. 'Most business is done through a middleman. I'm only an employee around here. They know I've got no personal axe to grind, not having a stake in the business.'

Jackie loosed off a few more choice oaths and began marching up and down the room. 'How much they offering? ... not that I'm interested!' he added hastily.

'Thirty thousand ... in cash, no questions asked. That's pretty good, considering none of the premises actually belong to you, only the wreck of the boat.'

Stott snorted derisively. 'Thirty grand! ... they must be joking. It's worth forty, fifty thousand any day, maybe more.'

Thor shrugged. 'Not if all the customers get their heads punched every night.'

Stott's face darkened immediately. 'I'll beat them ... Joe's getting half a regiment of. lads in tonight. Papagos will have to start compensating widows and orphans if he sends in any more hoodlums!'

'And how long do you think your licence will last if that sort of thing begins? ... it's none too safe now, after last night.'

Jackie swung around and grabbed Thor by the shoulder. 'I don't get you, mister,' he snarled. 'Every angle I mention gets the ice treatment from you ... you seem to want me out of business. Have they offered you a better job when they take over?'

Hansen pulled away and retreated around the settee away from Jackie. He took a deep breath – the crunch was about to come.

'Are you going to talk to them or not? They'll meet you anywhere in County Durham before tomorrow night. There's a draft contract all ready. You can take it to Lupin to get it vetted, or take him with you. There's no conveyancing of property to be done; the money could be in your hand by tonight.'

Jackie pointed a shaky finger at Thor, his face blazing with anger. 'You'd better get out and stay out, Hansen … I always trusted you, but you've gone and stabbed me in the back, damn you. Clear out, while I still haven't laid a hand on you!'

Hansen stood his ground. 'All right, Jackie, if you want it the hard way. I did know Papagos and Casella before this and I've gone along with them in this business … they've offered me a sixth share to be their manager. But I still think you've shot your bolt here and you won't get another good offer – or any offer, come to that.'

A torrent of foul language flowed over the Dane, but he stood unmoved, though he kept a wary eye on Jackie's big fists. When the storm died down for want of breath, he cut in with his ace.

'I didn't want to do this, but I'm going to force you to see sense.'

'You are! With what, a Bren gun?' yelled Jackie derisively.

'No … with Geordie Armstrong,' replied Thor quietly.

Jackie's low forehead wrinkled in perplexity. 'What the hell are you talking about?'

'Geordie Armstrong,' repeated Hansen. 'You and Joe killed him. I know and I can prove it – to the police, if I'm driven to it.'

Stott stared at him in sheer disbelief. He laughed, nervously now. 'Don' gimme that bull! What *sort* of proof?'

'All his clothes – in a plastic bag, with a piece of scrap iron in the bottom … and wallet, diary, the lot – probably with your fingerprints on them.'

There was a silence that could almost be felt.

'I don't believe you,' hissed Jackie at last. His face had

gone into mottled patches – a mixture of scared pallor and rage about to explode.

'The police will believe it. That dim idiot Joe dropped Geordie's clothes over the quayside on to a mud bank. I saw him do it, and when the tide went down, I picked them out. So unless you sell, I'll give you away to the law.'

He saw Jackie's amazement begin to kindle into blind rage and felt that discretion was the better part of valour.

'Here's Papagos's phone number – ring any time.'

He dropped a card over the back of the settee and left the flat almost at a run. He was no coward, but saw no benefit in staying to be mauled by an ex-professional fighter.

Jackie almost went after him, but turned his rage on to the furniture instead. Some minutes later, when he had righted the chairs and collapsed into one with his head in his hands, Joe Blunt came into the flat.

Unsuspectingly, he began to offer his clumsy apologies for the fiasco on the previous night, when his handpicked thugs had failed so miserably.

Jackie waved him down wearily. 'Forget it, Joe. We got something a lot worse to worry about now.'

He managed to get the facts of Thor's betrayal through Joe's thick skull and to convey the acute danger they were both in. The old sparring partner's reaction was typical. 'Shall I go after him and smash him?' he asked simply.

Jackie shook his head. 'There's been too much of that already, Joe. That wouldn't get rid of Thor's evidence against us.'

'How d'yer know he wasn't just bluffing, boss?'

Jackie scowled at him. 'Then how would he know it was in a plastic bag weighted with scrap?' he demanded. 'You were a bloody fool!' he added bitterly.

Joe cringed, his little red-rimmed eyes watery. 'I didn't know the flaming tide would leave it high and dry, did I? And who would 'a thought Hansen would be sneaking around there that time o' night?'

'No use crying over spilt milk … I'm damned if I'll be beaten by this. It took us years to build up this business. I'm not flogging it at the say-so of a couple of wop mobsters!'

'What we gonna do, then?'

'Get that bag of clothes back and destroy 'em. Hansen won't have a thing against us without them. The Papagos crowd I can deal with my own way.'

Even Joe's dim wits saw some sense in this.

'Where's he got the stuff, I wonder?'

'In his flat, up in Jesmond, I'll bet. He'll be away this afternoon, supposed to be going down to Middlesbrough again. I just gave him the sack, but knowing him, he won't take any notice till he gets it in writing or summat – or a poke on the nose, more likely!'

At two o'clock that afternoon, the white Mercedes drew up around a corner some yards from the old terrace house where Thor Hansen had a self-contained flat on the second floor, with a garage at the rear. The two men from the Rising Sun first reconnoitred this from the back lane.

'His car ain't there,' said Joe, peering through a dusty window pane. The Rover was not there, but it was not in Middlesbrough either, being only a few hundred yards away, having a routine service at a garage.

They went back to the front of the house and went through the unlocked front door and up the stairs to the second floor. At the top of the stairs was another door fitted with a Yale lock.

Their mode of entry was simplicity itself. They stood in front of the door, Jackie lifted his right foot and Joe Blunt his left.

'One – two – three!' chanted Stott and, on the 'three', two great feet with almost thirty stone behind them, crashed against the door below the lock.

It flew open as if it had been dynamited and the two men staggered inside with the momentum.

In the hallway, Jackie waved Joe towards the nearest door on the right, while he hurried to the one on his left.

It was a large bedroom, containing a double bed.

The bed contained Thor Hansen and Laura Levine, both sitting bolt upright at the noise. They were naked to the waist and Hansen's arm was still wrapped around the girl's shoulders.

Jackie stood transfixed for a second, whilst a red mist exploded in front of his eyes.

The singer gave a piercing scream and dived beneath the rumpled bedclothes as Stott charged across the room yelling obscenities. The Dane shouted with fear and struggled to get out of bed to escape the onslaught.

Jackie reached the bed in a couple of elephantine strides and dragged him out by the arm on to the floor. Completely berserk, he began kicking the naked body with frenzied blows from his heavy shoes.

Laura surfaced again and began screaming at the top of her voice, clawing her way across the bed to try and scram Jackie into leaving her lover alone.

Joe Blunt, attracted by the rumpus, lumbered into the room and across to the bedside, but before he could wrap himself around Jackie, the maddened ex-boxer had landed a dozen heavy blows with his feet to the Dane's head and chest.

Joe dragged him back, collecting a few punches in the process. Laura, heedless of her nakedness, was spitting and sobbing at Stott as she tried to take his eyes out with her painted fingernails.

'For Chrissake, boss, lay off!' panted Joe. 'We're in bad enough as it is.'

He managed to pull Jackie far enough away for Hansen's body to be out of range of Stott's flailing feet.

Laura, sobbing more than ever, slid down onto the floor

and crouched over Thor. His face was covered in blood as he lay curled up like an embryo. Great weals and grazes scarred his shoulders and chest as he lay as still as death.

Her hands trembled over his face and body. 'He's dead – you've killed him, you great bastard!' she mumbled incoherently through her sobs.

Jackie suddenly stopped struggling and stood trembling. Joe let him go and dropped down beside the woman on the carpet.

'Get some bloody clothes on, for God's sake,' he muttered, pushing her aside.

He turned Hansen over onto his back. The manager's left arm flopped limply to the floor and his jaw dropped, the eyes staring blankly at the ceiling.

Joe stood up slowly. 'You've done it again, Jackie … he's gone!'

Laura huddled the counterpane about herself and fell back to the floor, cradling Thor's bloody face against her bosom.

'Get an ambulance, you swine … get a doctor!' she moaned.

Joe pulled at Jackie's arm. 'Let's get outta here, boss. We don't need no bag of clothes now – you've done enough here to get you a life sentence, without worrying about Geordie!'

Emergency seemed to have stimulated Joe Blunt's brain, whereas Jackie appeared to be mentally paralyzed for the moment, now that the frenzy had worn off. Joe dragged him to the door and slowly the club owner began to return to normal.

Laura was still screaming for a doctor when they left the flat and got back to the Mercedes without incident.
'Back to the club, collect some clobber, then we'll have to lay low,' muttered Stott – the first coherent words he had uttered since he had fallen on the unfortunate Dane.

The drive back to the Bigg Market was made in

145

complete silence, but at the end of it, Jackie seemed outwardly normal.

He ran up to the flat, threw some clothes into a case and collected all the money he could lay his hands on, amounting to a few hundred pounds.

'What now?' demanded Joe, subsiding into his habitual doltish bewilderment, now that Jackie had taken over the initiative again.

Stott started the Mercedes, drove it into his garage behind the club and hustled Joe out again. 'Now we go find a cab!' he snapped in his best gangster tones. 'We collect Abel Lupin in Durham and then go through to Darlington. We got a date with some spot cash!'

At almost exactly the same time that Thor Hansen's front door was being smashed down, another less violent illegal entry was taking place in Benwell, in the West End of the city.

In the early hours of that morning, Alec Bolam had gone storming back to the Bigg Market to look for his daughter, but no one could or would tell him where Freddie Robson lived, so Bolam spent the rest of the night going around the home addresses of the band, the barmaids, and Herbert Lumley, in an attempt to find Freddie's whereabouts.

None of them knew and Alec, almost frantic with worry and frustration, got every beat man and motor patrol in the city to keep a lookout for the guitarist and his daughter. He drove around endlessly himself, checked all the night taxi services, but without success.

At six in the morning, he gave up and went home, to face his wife. At first their mutual distress formed a bond between them but, before breakfast time, Vera had got around to blaming him for the whole affair and by eight o'clock, he had rushed out again.

With Jimmy Grainger to help him, he stepped up the

search and eventually ran the organist to earth. He gave Bolam an address in Westerhope, on the outskirts of the city and a futile hour was wasted in discovering that Robson had left this address six months before.

Not until noon did they hit on the idea of trying the Electricity Board.

A phone call confirmed that the Board were willing to help trace a missing 'witness' and the two detectives went to dig through the files of the accounts office.

They ended up with a list of fifteen 'F. Robsons' living in areas likely to shelter the guitar player and on the ninth attempt at door-knockers, they struck lucky. At a dull red-brick house in Benwell, they found three bells at the side of the front door, one marked 'Robson'.

As Bolam peered at them, the door opened and a stout woman appeared with a shopping basket.

'Who yer lookin' for, pet?'

'Does a Freddie Robson live here, mum?'

'Aye – upstairs. You from the Assistance?'

'That's right … is he the fiddler from the Rising Sun?'

'Don' know where he works, hinny, but I've had te stop him playing his guitar over my living room ceiling.'

Bolam nodded his thanks and plunged up the stairs with Jimmy.

At the top of the stairs, the sounds of Radio One came through a door. Without hesitation, Alec pushed open the door and walked in.

He faced an astounded Freddie and his own daughter across a small room. They were sitting at a table cluttered with dirty cups, empty milk bottles and the remains of a sliced loaf wrapped in paper. Betty was wearing a man's dressing gown tightly belted around her waist. Her bare feet stuck out under the table and her hair was tangled about her face. The thin, freckled musician had on only a vest and tight black jeans.

In the background was a tumbled single bed.

Bolam took all this in with a single glance. His face was like granite. 'Come on, Betty, your mother wants a word with you.' She sat transfixed, her button-like mouth slightly agape. 'Sergeant Grainger, take this man into custody – charge him with abduction and obstructing the police. That'll do for a start.'

A grim wink passed between the two police officers. Jimmy, with an unconcealed grin of pleasure, grabbed Robson's arm. 'Get your togs on, laddie— we're off on a "trip" … my sort, this time!'

As he touched Freddie, the girl was galvanized into action. She leapt up and gave Jimmy a resounding smack in the face. 'Leave him alone, you great bully,' she yelled.

Then, to Alec's surprise, she ran around the table to her father and buried her head against his chest and began sobbing her heart out.

Jimmy, ruefully rubbing his cheek, propelled Freddie across the room, grabbed his shirt and jacket from a chair and stood over him while the guitarist struggled into them.

'I'll take him down to the police box on the corner and ring for a car,' said Grainger, with another wink, 'I'll leave you in peace to be getting along home.'

He jerked the cowed Freddie into motion and vanished down the stairs.

'Bolam awkwardly massaged the back of Betty's neck. 'Come on, now, pet, get your things … we'll get home, it'll be all right.'

'Don't tell Mum,' she blubbered into his waistcoat.

'Don't fret … it'll be our secret – that part of it.'

'I'm sorry I hit Jimmy like that,' she sniffed.

Women are bloody queer, thought Bolam.

Half an hour later, his explanations to Vera were interrupted by the telephone.

'Jimmy here, sir – they've been looking all over for us. Jackie Stott's done it again – put the boot into Thor

Hansen; they doubt if he'll live!'

Bolam felt as if the world was going a bit too fast for him. 'Where is he … what happened?' he spluttered.

'The singer from the Rising Sun sprung it – she rang nine-nine-nine for an ambulance. The crew rang the police when they got to the flat in Jesmond. He was alive, but only just and the doctors don't think he's going to last. They're all up at the General Hospital now.'

'I'm on my way – where are you?'

'At the West End station. I'll see you in the Admission Room.'

Bolam beat all records back to the West End of the city. He found Jimmy sitting in the Casualty Department, talking to Laura Levine. She wore no make-up and her face was pale and hard-looking.

'I can't say it all again,' she said huskily. Bolam beckoned Grainger away to hear the gist of her statement.

'She was in bed with Hansen at his flat, about two o'clock … Joe Blunt and Jackie bust the door open, then Jackie came into the bedroom, hauled Hansen out of bed and started to kick the hell out of him. Then they scarpered – simple as that.'

Bolam looked dubious.

'Something fishy about this. Jackie wouldn't go there in the middle of the day, and take Joe with him, just to play gooseberry on a woman. She say any more?'

Jimmy shook his head.

They went back to Laura.

'It seems touch and go for him, Miss Levine. I'm sorry to have to insist at a time like this, but I must have the whole story. Jackie Stott has got to be found – have you any idea where he might be?'

The girl shook her head listlessly. 'In hell, I hope … no, I don't know where he is.'

Grainger had already sent a patrol car to the Bigg Market; they had radioed back that the Rising Sun was deserted, but that the white Mercedes was still in the garage there. A general call was out for Stott and Joe Blunt, but no reports had yet come in. Bolam stared at Laura and hardened his attitude. After all, the woman was not a relative of the victim, only a bedfellow, by all accounts.

'Why did Stott break in to Hansen's place? Surely he didn't know you were there?'

Laura sighed. 'If Thor dies, Jackie will be charged with murder, that right?'

Bolam nodded. The singer seemed to be trying to make her mind up about something.

'Well, it won't make any difference, because Jackie is already a killer.'

Bolam's chin came up with a jerk. This sounded like the break to end all breaks. 'You mean Geordie Armstrong?'

She nodded, then the whole story came out. Once her tongue was loosened, there was a flood of words, which Bolam made no attempt to check … it could be edited later.

Everything that Thor Hansen had told her about Jackie mistaking Geordie as her lover, about his deal with Papagos and Casella, and the really juicy bit about finding Geordie's clothes in the river – it all tumbled out.

Alec Bolam began to hear birds singing in his brain and felt as if he had won the pools.

'Could Jackie have been looking for the bag of clothes, I wonder?' broke in the astute Jimmy Grainger.

Laura nodded. 'Possibly – they were locked in the boot of his car. It's being serviced in a garage in Osborne Road.'

Bolam was exultant, but there were urgent things to do.

'We'll want you to repeat all this in the form of a statement, but we'll get you over to the West End Station for that.'

Leaving her to wait for news of Hansen's condition, they sped back to Headquarters.

'We've got the whole damned crowd … Jackie, Joe, and the yobs from London … this evidence will shop the Greek and his pal for conspiracy at the very least.'

Jimmy Grainger was exuberant, but Bolam was more cautious.

'Let's hope that Hansen lives, then … he's the star witness; all her stuff is hearsay.'

'Not the bit about the clothes in the boot of his car?'

'That's your first job,' snapped Alec, swinging the car into the Headquarters' yard. 'Get a set of keys and go out to Jesmond to open the boot of that Rover.'

Jimmy shot off while Alec hurried to MacDonald's office to report on the dramatic turn of events. The chief had already heard an outline of the affair in Jesmond and was impatiently waiting for more details.

Bolam told the full story that he'd had from Laura Levine.

'It sounds as if Stott and Blunt actually think that the Dane is already dead,' said MacDonald thoughtfully. 'Both Joe and the girl said that he was dead before the ambulance arrived. Anyway, get a general call out to all forces. Watch ports and airports, that sort of thing.' He looked at the clock on the wall. 'He's been gone over an hour now, not a sign of him. Wonder where he'll make for?'

At that moment, Jackie, Joe and Abel Lupin, who knew nothing of the afternoon's events, were walking into the railway station at Durham City. The two men from Newcastle had arrived in a hire car at his office, and dragged Lupin off with them to do the legal business with the Greek and Sicilian down in Darlington. Lupin wondered why there was all the urgency, but Jackie managed to fob him off with excuses. By half past four, they were safely hidden in the hotel in Darlington, away from the increasingly watchful eyes of the Durham Constabulary.

A few moments after Bolam had made his escape from the chief superintendent's room, a jubilant Jimmy Grainger arrived back at Headquarters.

He carried a large polythene bag stuffed with slightly mouldy clothing. After it had been photographed and fingerprinted, they turned it out on a table in Alec's room and found a complete set of underclothes, shirt, suit and shoes.

The shirt was torn over the left side of the chest and it and the vest were stained with watery blood.

'Here's his wallet – no cash in it,' said Jimmy.

They went through the pockets carefully and laid everything out ready for dispatch to the forensic laboratory. At the bottom of the bag was a rusty piece of angle iron; the outside of the plastic was streaked with dried mud.

MacDonald came along to see it. 'Problem number one … find Joe and Jackie. Have we checked the bus stations and railway?'

They had been contacted, but no sign of the two fugitives had been found. The idea of questioning all the taxi men frankly had not occurred to the detectives, as they assumed that the two men would want to put a long distance between themselves and Newcastle, and a cab seemed an unlikely way of doing it.

By late afternoon, every policeman in Number Two Police District from the Scottish border down to mid-Yorkshire was on the lookout for Stott and Joe Blunt.

Copies of their prison photographs were hastily being printed for circulation and all other police forces were notified of the search. The Metropolitan Police were contacted with a view to watching any trains or long-distance buses arriving at the London termini from the North.

By early evening, Thor Hansen had had several holes drilled in his skull by the surgeons and a large blood clot removed. As he was still deeply unconscious, the doctors remained non-committal about his chances of survival.

Laura Levine had been taken to the West End Divisional Station and questioned more minutely by Alec Bolam. Significantly, he began by cautioning her with the classic old formula 'anything you say will be taken down and may be used in evidence'.

This did not seem to affect her in any way … she was in a state of dull apathy, her mind on the shaven-headed patient who lay inert in the hospital across the road. In an almost inaudible monotone, she gave an even more detailed account of the affair than before.

'Have you any idea at all where Stott may have run to?' persisted Bolam.

She shook her head wearily. 'Possibly London. He had a few contacts there, mainly old pals from his fighting days.'

Alec took down some addresses she gave him to add to the list to be checked. 'Anywhere else?'

The singer thought for a moment. 'He used to go to Ireland a lot … holidays and that. Maybe he fancies running there.'

'How much money would he be likely to have on him?'

Alec was thinking of sea or air fares for the two men.

'Quite a packet. He always carried a roll of notes, just to impress people when he flashed them. Then there would be a big cash float in the club, for the croupiers every night. That would be kept in the safe in his flat at the Rising Sun.'

'About how much?'

'At least a couple of hundred quid.'

Bolam sighed. The safe in the Bigg Market club had

been found open, with nothing inside but ledgers.

'Has he got a gun?' was the next question.

She shook her head decisively. 'He wasn't that sort. Always boasted that he could do more damage with his fists.'

'Or his feet,' added Bolam grimly.

The girl's eyes suddenly filled with tears and she nodded jerkily.

'These protection boys – Papagos and Casella – did you see them at any time?'

'Only when they came to the club – Jackie threw them out.'

'But you say Hansen went to see them yesterday in Darlington, to fix this blackmail of Stott over the bag of clothes?'

She bit her lip and for the first time began to see that she and her boyfriend – if he lived – were not going to get out of this scot-free.

'Do you know where they were staying?'

'No – Thor dropped me to look at the shops for half an hour. Must have been near the town centre, he wasn't gone long.'

She seemed to have no more to tell him and he left her to make another pilgrimage to the hospital.

'What are we going to do about Papagos and Casella?' asked Jimmy with curiosity.

Bolam scratched his head. 'Leave that to Uncle Mac and the DPP. They're a tricky bunch of monkeys. We should have the drop on them this time, but let's see if Hansen is going to be able to speak first.'

They drove away from the station, wondering where the devil to start looking for Jackie Stott and Joe Blunt.

At six o'clock that evening, the two men in question walked warily out of the hotel in Darlington and made their way to a small car hire firm in a back street.

154

Abel Lupin had left them some time earlier, to catch a train back to Durham; he little suspected that he had been sitting with two wanted men these past few hours.

While Joe Blunt went into the car rental depot, Jackie waited in the yard and thought about the transaction he had just made with the Soho crime kings. The Greek had unflinchingly stuck to his price of thirty thousand pounds. Jackie fumed and raved for a time, but Papagos was unmoving as the Rock of Gibraltar. If only he had known that several thousand police were outside looking for Jackie, his price – if any at all –would have been far lower. Stott was only too well aware of this to be in a bargaining position and eventually he had to capitulate.

Abel Lupin protested loud and long about the skimped legal formalities, but had to agree with Papagos that the draft agreement he produced was perfectly binding for all its brevity.

In essence, it transferred all the stock, equipment, staff contracts and goodwill of Jackie's business interests to Papagos for the cash sum of thirty thousand pounds.

The contract was signed and witnessed, then the Greek produced a suitcase filled to the brim with bundles of five-pound notes.

'Here you are, sixty bundles of a hundred notes each … check it if you like, but I wouldn't twist you. I might burn your place down and Bruno here might stick a knife in your ribs, but I wouldn't stoop to fiddle you over cash.'

He said this half in jest, but Jackie believed him. He was past caring, anyway. When Joe Blunt hefted the case and stood up Jackie was already on his way to the door.

'I thought Thor Hansen would have been in on this,' said Kostas Papagos.

Jackie's brow darkened. 'We don't exactly see eye to eye – not since I found he was a stoolie for you!' he growled. Stott was no great actor, but he carried this off

155

quite well.

Leaving the Greek and his partner with their makeshift contract, the two Tynesiders had slipped out into the gloom with their precious case, to risk the hazard of the Darlington streets. Now Jackie waited impatiently for Joe to fix up the car, keeping his back to the gateway leading to the police infested roads.

To his relief, a three-year-old Vauxhall with his henchman behind the wheel appeared from the garage and stopped to pick him up.

'Right – back to Newcastle, the long way around!'

Joe set off on a devious route that more than doubled the distance, going away from the Great North Road into the moorland country that led westwards to the Pennines. They aimed for Bishop Auckland, Tow Law and the more pastoral parts of the upper Tyne valley, to circle north and approach the big city from the opposite direction.

During the long journey, Jackie took the opportunity to count the bundles of notes in the dim light from the dashboard.

'That bloody wop was right – there's exactly thirty grand here – not ten bob more or less!' he grunted to Joe, whose piggy eyes were squinting ahead at the deserted road.

'It looks OK?' growled the old sparring partner.

Jackie sniffed. 'I'll lay evens that it's "hot" … all used and dirty notes. But the numbers are all over the place, none consecutive, so it's sure to be untraceable.'

'Think they'll be all right?' persisted Joe, in a worried voice, swinging his big head to look at the cash.

'Keep yer flaming eyes on the road,' snapped Jackie. 'You get us in the ditch now and we won't be needing any bloody money for the next fourteen years or so.'

He clicked the case shut and dropped it between his legs. 'Yes, it'll do … we'll be changing it bit by bit all through Holland and down France into Spain.'

Joe digested this in silence. Then he said, 'I haven't got a passport. Never bin outta the country before, see.'

Jackie sighed. 'I said I'd fix all that, din't I? We take the boat into Amsterdam and I contact this chap I know, runs a casino there. He'll flog the boat for us, fix us some fake passports and get us a good car with the proceeds. He's a real villain, do anything for me – I knew him in the war.'

Joe still sounded dubious.

'Then what we do? Neither of us speak the lingo. We'll get picked up, sure as hell.'

Jackie snapped at him. 'Bloody moaner, you are! Look, that boat of mine will cross the North Sea as if it was a duck pond. We'll be in the south of Spain inside a week.'

'Then what?' Joe sounded unconvinced.

'Tangier, boy! I had a holiday there, a coupla years back – smashing place, plenty of graft, no questions asked, no extradition. We can grow ourselves a couple of beards, nobody'll know us from Adam. With this thirty thousand we can get set up in a little club. Start modest, we could clean up a fortune in a year or two. Better off than doing fourteen years in the nick, I tell you.'

They drove on in silence for some miles while Jackie's brain tried to work out all the angles and possible snags in his bid for freedom and one of the first he spotted was fuel.

'Stop at the next filling station,' he ordered and, at a garage in a lonely hamlet, they drew up at the petrol pumps. After having some in the tank of the Vauxhall, Stott asked the attendant if he had any empty oil drums that could be filled with diesel fuel. 'Need it for our farm generator up at Allendale,' he explained.

The man produced two ten-gallon drums and filled them from the DERV pump, Jackie managing to stow them in the boot. At another garage ten miles further on, they repeated the process, this time putting three drums on the back seat.

'That should be enough to get the *Bella* to America, let alone the Dutch coast,' exaggerated Stott in satisfaction, after they had driven off. 'Her main tank is full – that's fifty gallons – and I've already got a couple of spare drums aboard.'

Eventually, they approached Newcastle and began cautiously to enter the suburbs from the west. Jackie took over the driving, telling Joe to lie flat on the floor at the back. The police might be looking for two men leaving Newcastle, but Stott calculated that they would be much less interested in one man entering the city. He found an old pair of sunglasses in the glove compartment and, after pushing the lenses out, wore the empty frames as an apology for a disguise.

Sedately, they travelled through the streets without challenge, the Vauxhall making its way steadily towards Scotswood, about two miles upstream from the bridges between Newcastle and Gateshead.

Here, at a dismal mooring between two factories, a dozen private craft dozed on the black water. Some were lifeboat conversions, used mainly by fishing parties, and others were proper motor cruisers.

The biggest and best was Jackie's boat, the *Bella*. She was not a heavy-weather boat but, as long as the present weather held, she could cope with the crossing to Holland.

Jackie ran the car down a lane between high walls and coasted quietly to the wharfside. The *Bella* was moored twenty yards from the bank, to be out of the reach of marauding children. There was a 'pram' dinghy belonging to one of the other boats tied to the quayside and within a few moments, Jackie had paddled out and hauled the cruiser to the wharf. The tide was high and the strong arms of the two ex-boxers soon dumped the oil drums down on to the deck.

Jackie's seafaring eye looked them over critically.

'Better lash them together on the after-part of the deck – they'll keep her bottom well down in the watter!'

He left Joe doing this while he reversed the Vauxhall well back into the shadows on the quay. When all was secure, they went into the cockpit and a moment later the whine of the electric starters and the splutter of the cold engines broke the late evening silence of the river.

The diesels fired and began to run smoothly as they warmed up. Jackie switched the navigation lights on and gently moved astern from the moorings, into the main stream of the Tyne.

'Cheerio, England – and bloody good riddance,' he muttered, patting the suitcase that lay on the locker alongside him.

Chapter Twelve

'Everything is going perfectly,' growled MacDonald. 'Hansen seems to be pulling through; we've got a solid case against everyone concerned – the only small point is that the two principals involved have vanished from the face of the blasted earth!'

He spoke through the window of his car, just before driving off from Headquarters. Bolam and Grainger stood outside and raised their hands in a salute of farewell as he drove away.

'He's right, you know … I didn't think those two thick bastards would have the savvy to keep out of sight as well as this,' said Jimmy, as they went back into the building.

'Jackie's not thick, not by a hell of a way,' corrected Alec. 'Granted, Joe Blunt is a bit of a zombie, but Stott's as cunning as they come. He's arrogant and vain and thinks he's too clever to be caught … but where the blazes *are* they?'

It was late evening by now and the two detectives went to the canteen for tea and biscuits. One of the photography sergeants was there and they began the inevitable discussion on the case.

'Where would *you* go if you were wanted for murder, Sam?' asked Jimmy.

'A long way abroad – South America or Canada, to join the Train Robbers,' said the other sergeant promptly.

'Come off it, Jackie's only got a few hundred quid, not a few million.'

'Well, anywhere abroad – you can get all over Europe for that sort of money.'

'The singer girl suggested Ireland,' put in Bolam, thoughtfully. 'We've asked for a special watch on the Irish packet terminals and the airports ... two big thugs like them could hardly go unnoticed.'

'The Met are keeping an eye on King's Cross and places like that, but it's a hell of a job to watch everywhere,' added Grainger.

'What about passports?' asked the photographer. 'Jackie's is missing from the safe, according to the Levine woman. Joe never had one, by all accounts.'

'They must be holed up somewhere – probably under our noses in Newcastle.'

'What about this taxi driver who says he took them to Durham this afternoon?'

'Beats me ... I can hardly believe it, to be honest,' sighed the chief inspector.

'The cabbie seemed definite enough, but why the hell would they pick Durham?'

There was a silence, broken only by munching and sipping.

Neither Bolam nor Jimmy felt like going home. They somehow felt that by staying on, they might charm events into going right for them. Alec had no particular wish to go back to face a barrage of questions from Vera about Betty's lost hours the previous night. The girl herself had become withdrawn and silent since she returned – the brief period of tenderness with her father had been short-lived but her infatuation with Freddie seemed to have vanished and Bolam prayed that the experience hadn't twisted her against men permanently.

He went back to his office, and for a time there was a brooding silence in the room, until it was broken by the clamour of the telephone.

'Leadbitter here – Tyne Division ... switchboard told me you were still in.'

'Ernie … what the dickens are you doing this time of night?'

'Changed shifts – doing a spell of nights while Andrews gets his haemorrhoids fixed … Jimmy Grainger rang up earlier today and left a message asking about tide times on the day Geordie Armstrong was killed.'

'That's right – we found the clothing and we wanted to check that it could have been retrieved at the time Hansen was supposed to have found it on the mud bank.'

The River Sergeant quoted some times over the phone and Alec jotted them down.

'No sign of them villains yet, sir?' asked Leadbitter, conversationally.

'Not a trace, Ernie … they're bound to surface sometime, though. We had a suggestion that they might have stowed away on a ship from the Tyne … any Dutch or German coasters in the river tonight?'

There was a silence, then a thoughtful voice came over the line. 'No-o, I can't think of any of the masters touching a job like that.' His voice became brisker. 'But look here, sir, I just ruddy thought of something! What about the *Bella*?'

Bolam was in a fog. 'Bella? … who the hell's she?'

Leadbitter sounded really agitated now. 'No, the *Bella* … Jackie's own boat, sir … a big twin-screw diesel.'

Bolam felt a pulse suddenly begin to beat in his neck.

'He's got his own boat? … Christ, why didn't someone tell me!' He calmed himself with an effort. 'Ernie, look … tell me about it.'

'That's about all to tell … a big cruiser, best part of forty foot. He only bought it last summer. Moored up the river.'

'Where?'

'At the Scotswood pool … beyond the Vickers factory.'

Alec stood still, holding the phone. 'I'll be straight down, Ernie. Probably nothing in it, but we'd better check.

Can you take me up there, just in case? They may have been there, or they may be aiming to hide out on it. I'll be with you in five minutes, get a boat standing by.'

He jiggled the phone button and rang the Information Room, requesting the nearest motor patrol to go to the moorings at Scotswood. Then, scooping up Jimmy, he took a CID car to go down to the River Police Station at the Swing Bridge.

Halfway there, the 'beep-beep' standby signal of the radio was replaced by the impassive voice of Information Room calling them.

'L-K to Q-6 … L-K to Q-6.'

Bolam snatched up the handset. 'Q-6 to L-K … over.'

'G-8 wishes talk-through with you … go ahead, G8.'

An agitated Geordie voice came through direct from the police car that Bolam had sent down to Scotswood. 'G-8 to Q-6 … that you, Mr Bolam?'

'Yes – what's the panic?'

'That boat, sir – the *Bella*. She's gone!'

Alec's heart seemed to rise and stick somewhere below his chin. 'Are you sure you've got the right one?'

'Yessir … I've got the local PCs here in the Panda van … they know the boat. She was here yesterday. They check up for vandalism and that. It was definitely here then, it's the biggest one on the moorings.'

Alec swore into the radio, momentarily paralyzed by the news.

The patrolman spoke again, almost apologetically. 'One thing, Mr Bolam … there's a Vauxhall car parked nearby, in a queer spot. Radiator's still warm. There's a sticker on the window says "Salter's Car Hire, Darlington".'

Alec got a grip of himself. 'Right, thank God for something. Get through to Information to check on who hired it.'

'Will do – G-8 out.'

The CID car was in Pilgrim Street by now, with Jimmy driving and bursting with anticipation.

'Step on it, Jimmy … it looks damned likely that Jackie has made a run for it in his boat.'

The Austin shot forward to rip around into Market Street and race down the elegant slope of Grey Street.

'Surely they're not going to risk running abroad in a motor boat?'

'Jackie was a sailor – this *Bella* seems to be a big, powerful craft. Why the hell didn't somebody tell us he had a bloody boat?'

They tore down the steep hill of Dean Street towards the Tyne, screeched around the bends near the Guildhall and shot across the deserted Swing Bridge to the old red brick police station.

Almost before Jimmy had stopped, Bolam was out and was clattering into the building. In the front office he found Leadbitter and two constables drinking the inevitable tea before a glowing stove.

'Jackie's on the run in his blasted boat,' he blurted. 'Has anything passed here?'

The river policeman looked at him incredulously.

'Not a thing in the last hour – the ash hopper was the last craft through the bridge,' said Ernie.

He hurried to the window and looked out into the segment of river that lay between the High Level and Swing bridges.

'Nothing to be seen … they can't have passed down.'

'Could you see a boat as small as that? He might have his lights out,' said Bolam.

'He'd not risk getting stopped just for that … I reckon he'd leave 'em on. No, I'll swear nothing's gone down since the hopper.'

'Got a boat ready?'

'Right at the door – we were going on patrol when you phoned.'

He grabbed his hat and made for the door, followed by the phlegmatic Horace, his crewman once again. Bolam and Jimmy hurried after them, Bolam turning as he reached the door to speak to the duty constable.

'Will you ring Information, tell them that Stott and Blunt are thought to be on the run in a boat – inform Chief Superintendent MacDonald. Tell them we'll radio further information as soon as we have any.'

He ran after the others and clambered down slimy wooden steps to the lapping water. Leadbitter held the launch close to the jetty for him and as soon as he was aboard, Horace gunned the engine and swung off upriver.

The wind had freshened a lot during the last hour and the policemen stood huddled on the open after-deck, collars turned up and hands deep in their pockets, as they stared ahead at the river.

'Have to take a chance on going upstream – but I'll swear nothing's come down past us,' yelled Leadbitter against the noise of the Perkins engine at their feet. 'It's about fifteen minutes run from here to the moorings.'

'What if he has gone through already?' shouted Bolam.

Ernie moved towards the cabin. 'I'll call up Shields and warn them.'

They roared up river while the sergeant radioed the distant River Headquarters at South Shields. A few moments later he was back.

'Mike Milburn is on patrol halfway down the river, somewhere around Wallsend. Control have given him the story – nothing has passed him down there, he says.'

'So Jackie is still on the river?'

'Unless he left hours ago – though I'm sure someone on patrol would have noticed him. That *Bella* is a big, fine boat. You don't get many pleasure craft on the river in December!'

They were interrupted by a shout from Horace. 'Navigation lights! … just beyond Dunston Staithes!'

They all peered ahead and twinkling faintly against the gloomy background, they eventually picked out two lights, the higher one yellow and other red. The hull was invisible at that distance.

'Take her over that side, Horace,' commanded Leadbitter. The police launch began slanting across the river to the downstream channel and the distance between the two craft rapidly lessened.

Both Horace and Ernie Leadbitter shouted simultaneously. 'It's her – it's the *Bella*!'

'That high cabin and the canvas canopy give her away – nothing else like it up this part of the river,' hollered the sergeant excitedly.

The gap between them lessened every second.

'What the hell do we do now?' asked Jimmy, 'Jump aboard with cutlasses in our teeth?'

'We've got to catch her first,' shouted Leadbitter. 'That boat can run rings around us when it comes to speed. Our engine is governed down to twelve knots in case we hit floating wreckage.'

He stood to the cabin entrance and shouted at Horace. 'Come up ahead of her and try to force her in towards the bank. Don't give her any sea-room and for Gawd's sake don't let her get abeam of us or she'll be away like a dose of salts.'

The launch swerved to port, then swung back so that the two boats seemed to be racing together on a collision course.

'We'll only have a second or two to get aboard,' yelled Ernie. 'Horace will try to slide up past her as we touch. Get ready to jump for it!'

The three police officers crouched along the gunwale, but their nervous tension was wasted.

Horace tried to cross the path of the *Bella* at the last moment to force her to give way whilst he slid alongside, but Jackie and his twin Volvo engines were too good for him. He had been running down river at much less than full power and as Horace got into position, Stott flicked open his throttles. The big white boat fairly leapt forwards, swinging away from the police boat at the same time.

Horace's craft was completely outclassed and in seconds, he was left staring at an empty stretch of river.

'Hang on!' he yelled and cranked the wheel full over. Under full power, the black launch lurched as she came about, but by the time they were facing downstream again, the *Bella* was a hundred yards ahead and pulling away rapidly.

'We haven't a hope in hell of catching her now,' Leadbitter roared, 'Let's hope Milburn has better luck … he's got a slightly newer boat than this old tub, though it still won't come near the *Bella* for speed.'

He dived back to the radio to give Control the news and to offer Mike Milburn a few words of advice on how to tackle Stott's craft.

'What the hell are we going to do now?' yelled Jimmy Grainger, his teeth juddering with cold.

Bolam huddled close to save his voice. 'Let's hope the big white chief in Headquarters can get something organized … at least we know where Jackie is now … we've flushed him out into the open … there's nowhere he can go except out to sea.'

Although the *Bella* had initially spurted ahead, she settled down to keep a steady distance from them, Stott soon finding that Horace's top speed was far below his own.

'He's throttled back,' observed Leadbitter, coming from the radio. 'Saving fuel and making sure he doesn't get holed by any of that flotsam … a canny sailor, Jackie must be.'

'Where's Milburn's boat now?' asked Bolam.

'Belting up from Wallsend – he's just passed Swan Hunter's shipyard. He says he's going to hide out behind the stern of a ship fitting out at Walker Naval Yard and wait for the *Bella* to come round the bend of the river at St Anthony's … then he can surprise her, he hopes.'

Their own boat was pounding along at full speed, but Stott kept the same lead on them.

'Only a hundred yards away, yet he might as well be in the Suez Canal for all we could do to him,' snarled Alec Bolam, huddled in the open cabin to keep away from the worst of the ever-freshening wind.

'If the weather keeps up like this, even yon *Bella*'s going to have a rough time once she gets beyond the pier heads,' observed Ernie Leadbitter.

'Let's hope to God she never gets that far to find out,' retorted the detective.

'What happens if Milburn fails to get aboard, like us?' asked Jimmy.

'Let's wait and work that out when it happens –'

The loudspeaker screwed to the windshield pillar rasped tinnily.

'Tynepol Control for *D for Dog* – Control calling *D for Dog*.'

Leadbitter went forward to take the handset out of the cubby and a moment later waved to Bolam to take it. 'Mr MacDonald is on the phone to Shields Headquarters – they can't talk through on this set. He wants to know what's going on.'

'I'll bet he does,' said Bolam, taking the instrument. 'Control, tell the chief superintendent that Stott's boat is on its way down driver. Our first interception failed, another is to be attempted shortly. Ask him to arrange alternative method of arrest if this fails.'

There was a pause, then acknowledgment before the radio went back to standby.

Bolam climbed out on to the open deck to join the other two, who had gone to stare once more after the fleeing *Bella*. He stood feet wide apart as the police launch went flat out down the dark river.

'Any sort of weapon on board?' he shouted over the roar of the engine in its box alongside them.

'Nothing – only the starting handle for that,' replied the sergeant, pointing.

'They're a tough pair, Jackie and Joe … and desperate. They've got nothing to lose now. They'll be facing a life sentence whatever happens, so we want to watch ourselves.'

'We got to get aboard first,' growled Ernie in disgust. 'If Mike Milburn manages it, he'll give 'em their money's worth – hard as bloody nails, he is.'

They were on a barren part of the river now, nearing St Anthony's Point.

'Wicker's Naval Yard is just around the corner,' called Leadbitter, 'There's a big cargo liner half-finished, moored on the north bank – Mike says he'll be lurking behind that.'

Around the bend, the cranes of the yard came into view, just visible against the glowing background of the Walker street lights. The *Bella* was still running easily ahead, cutting the corner as she moved from the right-hand channel towards the shipyard. The river had a wide bulge in it here, where the Danish passenger boats swung around during the summer months. The two launches were dwarfed for a few moments in the expanse of water.

'He's keeping to the middle, rather than the south bank,' observed Leadbitter in satisfaction. 'Gives Milburn a better chance to get near him as he goes past.'

The bulk of a fourteen thousand-ton cargo-passenger liner loomed up ahead. The light was slightly better here, and Bolam watched in fascination as the white motor cruiser passed the half-finished ship.

Suddenly, with an audible revving of the engine, a police launch shot out from the darkness under the cargo ship's stem and headed straight for the *Bella*.

Jackie Stott was almost caught by surprise.

'He's going to get him!' yelled Jimmy exultantly. The smaller black boat, headed slightly upstream, tried to come alongside bow to bow, as Horace had attempted further up river.

'He'll do it – he will!' shouted Ernie, standing up on the gunwale for a better view.

Milburn *almost* did it.

Jackie, caught unawares, opened his throttles at the last moment as the police launch suddenly appeared in front of him. He swung his wheel over and Milburn followed suit, then Jackie unexpectedly jerked back in the opposite direction.

By this time the two craft had almost closed and a second later the bows of the bigger one smashed a glancing blow against the police launch, followed by a side swipe as the turning flank hit her amidships.

'She's going over,' screamed Leadbitter. The black boat swayed up on its side, hesitated and then fell right over, it flat bottom glistening faintly in the dim light.

The white cruiser forged on, its bow crumpled well above the waterline, but otherwise undamaged.

'There's one of them!' yelled Bolam, leaning over the side as they came up to the wreck.

In seconds, Horace had brought their boat alongside the capsized launch and their small searchlight cut through the night. One wet constable was already clinging to the hull and a moment later, Milburn appeared, spitting water like a whale. They were hauled aboard and Horace opened up the throttles again. Mike Milburn, between bouts of teeth chattering, swore long, loud and fluently.

'N-nearly had the b-bastard – I don't think he rammed me deliberate, we both swung the same way together.'

Leadbitter miraculously produced two grey blankets from somewhere and wrapped the soaked officers in them as they stumbled down into the cabin.

'What happens now?' asked Milburn. 'We've got another boat waiting at Shields, but the same thing will happen to that – we're four to five knots behind the *Bella* for speed.'

Bolam swore. 'Haven't we got something faster? The only way to catch him is to follow him and come alongside.'

Leadbitter shrugged. 'The police have got nothing faster – we're not the bloody Navy, you know.'

Jimmy snapped his fingers. 'What about the Fisheries patrol boat – that minelayer. She'd run rings around him!'

'Or blow him 'oot the watter with her four-inch,' added Mike cynically.

'She went out on patrol yesterday, to chase Dutchmen away from British kippers,' Milburn's constable informed them.

'Let's try and get her,' muttered Bolam. 'If Stott gets out of the Tyne entrance into the sea, it'll be the only hope.'

He moved down to the front observation seat and grabbed the radio again. Before he could put through a message, it crackled throatily and began relaying a message from MacDonald.

The detective chief inspector finished with the radio and came back to Jimmy. 'Mac's rung the local naval wallah – he had the same idea as us about that Fisheries boat … but it's up on the coast north of Holy Island – take at least three hours steaming even assuming that the Admiralty would sanction its use.'

There was a gloomy silence.

'What about a helicopter?' asked Milburn.

Jimmy shook his head. He had a brother in the Air Force. 'They don't operate at night – and can you see Jackie letting them land a couple of blokes on his deck!'

Ernie Leadbitter suddenly slapped his hand on the engine casing. 'Got it! Why the hell didn't I think of it before – the *Vidette*! Gimme that radio!'

Twenty minutes later, the *Bella* passed the spot where Geordie Armstrong's body had been dumped a week earlier. In the wide, comfortable cockpit, Jackie stood at the wheel, a dimly lit instrument panel casting a faint glow on his grim features.

Joe Blunt came up from the cabin below with two mugs of coffee and set one down on the windscreen ledge in front of Stott.

'Pity we've been rumbled!' Joe muttered for the fourth time, 'If we could 'a made it out to sea, they'd have had no bleeding idea where we'd gone.'

Jackie shook his head. 'Couldn't be done – we have to pass Lloyd's hailing station at the end of the Fish Quay. They'd be bound to notice us – a pleasure boat going out to sea at midnight just before Christmas is a damned queer thing, fair play.'

Privately, his robust self-confidence was wearing a bit thin. He was going on because he couldn't turn back.

It would be obvious to the police that the only place he could be heading for was the nearest point on the continent. The foreign police would be tipped off and he now had no idea if he could manage to get ashore unseen. They had neither the fuel nor the seaworthiness to risk the crossing to Denmark and they were virtually committed to the southerly route across to Holland.

His only hope was that they might steal ashore at some deserted spot at night, though this meant abandoning the boat and losing the chance of selling it at Rotterdam to increase their funds. Still, at the moment he was more concerned with the present and getting clear of the Tyne.

'What's happening astern, Joe – those coppers still limping along after us?'

'There's two of them now,' reported Joe, using a pair of giant binoculars. 'Another launch has just come out from the South Shields side.'

'The same piddling little police boats?'

'Yes, they're running side by side.'

Jackie laughed and sucked down some coffee. 'If one can't catch us, two won't do any better.'

'Think we'll get clear now?'

'What's to stop us! The coppers haven't got guns – and they wouldn't be allowed to use 'em if they had … we're unarmed.'

Joe started aft again through the powerful binoculars. Suddenly he stiffened and swung around to focus on the place near where the dredger had scraped Geordie's body from the river bed.

'Christ, Jackie … there's a flaming big launch coming out – bigger than us!'

Stott swore and looked over his shoulder through the Perspex rear window of the canopy in the direction that Joe was pointing.

'The harbourmaster's launch – the *Vidette*. Hell and damnation, I never thought of her! Big forty-foot twin-screw job. She can give us a couple of knots at least!'

He leant forward and rammed both throttle levers forward. The *Bella* grumbled deep inside and the bow lifted as the screws dug harder into the water.

Joe continued to stare astern through the glasses. 'But she ain't a police boat … and anyway, she's turning up river!'

Jackie twisted around again to look. 'What the hell's she up to then?' he muttered suspiciously.

Joe followed the action anxiously through his binoculars. He soon saw what the plan was to be. The *Vidette* tore up the river to meet the two smaller police launches, then swung in a tight circle to come alongside one of them. The old pug saw several black figures leap aboard the big blue diesel launch and without a second's delay, she leapt ahead and forged down river in advance of the police boats.

'They've taken on some coppers – now she's coming after us like a bat outta hell!' yelled Joe in real alarm.

Stott anxiously groped for the throttle levers again, but they were hard against their stops. For a few minutes, the *Bella* seemed to be holding her lead on the *Vidette*, but as they passed the narrow gap between the hailing station and the pilot jetty, things began to change.

This was now virtually open sea and had been until the great granite piers had been built. Though it had been fairly calm in the sheltered narrows of the river, there was a stiff breeze in this great mile-long triangle of the Tyne entrance. A steep choppy sea began to slam into the stem of the *Bella* and she started to pitch badly.

The harbourmaster's boat was built for going out to sea in most weathers and her extra weight, length and freeboard made light of the sudden change in conditions as she followed the *Bella* out of the shelter of the river.

Jackie's boat was lurching and hammering and water began splashing in through the crumpled bows.

'They're gaining on us fast,' yelled Joe, as he stared astern through the spray. Before they were three-quarters of the way to the twin lighthouses at the ends of the piers, the *Vidette* was upon them.

Alec Bolam, Jimmy Grainger and the two River sergeants were standing ready on the port side of the *Vidette*. They clung firmly to the handrail running along the cabin roof as the powerful boat smashed through the choppy water in regular fountains of spray.

By the time they came up to the *Bella*, they were all as wet as Mike Milburn, who had been in the Tyne once that night but who on no account was going to be left out of the kill. His constable had hurt his shoulder when the second launch had capsized and Milburn had ordered him to stay on the other boat.

'If the four of us can't match those two, I'll give up me

pension,' he yelled as the bow of their launch came level with the pitching stern of the *Bella.*

In desperation, Jackie began weaving about to prevent them coming alongside, but all he succeeded in doing was to lose speed and control.

The elderly stolid helmsman of the *Vidette* countered every move of Stott's and inexorably, the two craft drew level. The other crewman of the harbourmaster's boat clung on to the drenched foredeck with a boat hook in one hand and as soon as he could, he made a snatch at the *Bella*'s rail and heaved so that the narrow gap momentarily vanished.

As Milburn and Bolam jumped, a flap in the side of the white cruiser's cockpit burst open and Joe Blunt erupted. He charged for the boat hook, trying to throw it off so that Jackie could shear away.

Jimmy and Leadbitter hurled themselves across the gap just before Joe kicked the hook from the seaman's hands. The two vessels separated at once, but the *Vidette* hung tenaciously within a few yards.

Joe swung round to face the four policemen. The boat was bucking and twisting worse than ever, especially as she was beginning to take in a lot of water through the damaged bow.

Everyone's anxieties were divided between the inevitable fight that was coming and the need to cling on to something merely to survive.

The chief inspector and three sergeants were crowded together on the tiny after-deck, most of which was cluttered with the oil drums, now grinding together ominously inside their lashings. Jimmy Grainger nearly fell overboard within seconds of arriving, but made a terrified grab at the flimsy side rail and hung there petrified for a moment.

Joe Blunt crouched like a great wet ape, one hand clamped on the cockpit handrail. He yelled something at them, but the wind and the noise of the sea and the engines carried it away. Leadbitter was nearest to him and the older sergeant bravely advanced on the ex-pugilist, going hand over hand along the rail. As he came level with the canopy, Joe suddenly jumped forward and gave Ernie Leadbitter a tremendous blow on the jaw from his ham-like fist.

The sergeant went down as if pole-axed and only a stanchion prevented him from rolling straight into the sea.

'Hold on, Ernie!' yelled Jimmy, who was next in line on the restricted combat area.

The deck alongside the cockpit was only a foot or so wide, a mere catwalk joining fore and after deck spaces. There was no hope of a broadside attack on Joe.

Grainger stepped over Leadbitter's groaning body and feinted at Joe with his left hand. Joe struck again and Jimmy automatically brought up both arms to shield himself. A lurch of the boat nearly threw both of them down – the blow landed on his elbow and nearly paralysed his arm, but he stumbled on and grabbed Joe around the waist, in a poor sort of rugby tackle.

'Watch out, for God's sake!' screamed Bolam from behind.

Jimmy now had no grip on the boat at all, both his arms being around Joe's thick belly. He tried making short-arm jabs into the older man's kidneys, but Joe seemed to be made of rock. The old boxer thumped the detective in the middle of the back, then, like the landlubber he was, made the fatal mistake of letting the rail go in order to force Jimmy's head back. The very next lurch of the *Bella* threw them clean over the flimsy rail into the sea, still locked in each other's grip. Milburn and Bolam looked wildly over the side as the two bodies flashed past, going astern at sixteen knots.

'The *Vidette* will get them!' yelled Milburn and even as he said it, the bigger launch dropped back and swung around, its searchlight blazing.

Alec and the sergeant dragged Ernie Leadbitter back on to the slightly wider space at the stern and propped him against the oil drums, hooking one arm through the lashings. He was conscious but dazed, managing to wave them feebly away.

'You'll be all right here, Ernie – hang on to these drums,' hollered Milburn into his ear, then followed Bolam back to the cockpit.

'You take the other side,' ordered the CID man and in a moment they were standing one each side of the closed flaps in the black canvas canopy.

Bolam was on the port side and could see Jackie dimly though the plastic side-screen. They were well clear of the river now and the only light came from the reflections of the dim navigation lamps and intermittently from the great beam of the North Pier lighthouse, now just ahead of them.

In the glow from the instrument panel, Jackie could be seen wrestling with the wheel as the *Bella* bucked and pitched in the choppy swell. He was on Bolam's side and the detective put his face to the flexible screen and yelled at the top of his voice.

'All right, Jackie – pack it in! Joe's gone and you can't get anywhere from here … turn her around and go back!'

The answer was a thunderous punch against the canvas, which caught Bolam on the forehead, making him see stars in the overcast sky.

'Right, if that's how you want it!' he retorted, his temper suddenly in flames.

Part of the canopy was a flap, held down by big press studs. He ripped this open, yelled across the roof to Milburn, then threw himself inside, virtually on top of Jackie Stott.

He collected a terrible punch in the first second, but managed to turn his head so that it landed on his neck instead of his face. The momentum of his entry made

Jackie stagger away from the wheel and Bolam, half-crazed with the pain in his neck, lashed out and caught Stott a lucky blow in the eye.

Though Jackie had had a hundred of these in his time, Alec Bolam was a powerful man and was not wearing boxing gloves. The blow shook Jackie and before he could recover, Milburn had clambered in from the other side and jumped on Stott from behind.

The *Bella*, with throttles wide open but no one at her wheel, careered around until she was in the trough of the waves. They were just passing through the pier entrance into the open sea and the rollers were coming straight across from Norway at them. It seemed touch and go whether she would capsize or crash into the granite wall of the lighthouse foundation, but Milburn, the sailor-policeman, was well aware of the danger.

'The wheel!' he screamed, 'swing her to starboard … the right, man!'

Mike forgot the niceties of rank in the heat of the moment and a second later, he forgot everything else, as Jackie broke free and landed him a terrible punch in the stomach.

As Bolam grabbed the helm, the other two men fell down the narrow steps leading to the cabin below. This gave him a few seconds respite, but he realized that Jackie would soon be on him again. He groped hazily for the throttles. The boat was almost touching the pier, the lighthouse above throwing its yellow beam twenty miles out to sea, indifferent to the drama at its feet.

Bolam was saved by the appearance of Leadbitter at the opening alongside. Shaken and grey – he was later found to have a fractured jaw – he stumbled in and grabbed the wheel, pushing Bolam in the direction of the two combatants.

Jackie was now rolling in the narrow companionway, on top of a vomiting Mike Milburn.

Bolam had gone far beyond caring about a clean fight. He jumped with both feet into the stairwell, landing his big brogues squarely on Jackie Stott's head.

The boxer, who was just getting up, crashed back against the floorboards and lay still.

The fight was over.

When Leadbitter brought the motor cruiser back into the lee of the north pier and the *Vidette* came alongside, Jackie was still unconscious.

The two police launches arrived, having made heavy weather of the trip across to the lighthouses. Horace came aboard and took over the controls of the *Bella* from the injured Leadbitter. Everyone else transferred to the *Vidette* which made the return trip looking like a hospital ship.

Jackie Stott began to groan himself awake after five minutes; Mike Milburn continued to retch for another ten. Ernie Leadbitter began to bleed from his injured mouth, while Joe Blunt and Jimmy Grainger were still incoherent with cold after their brief dip in the freezing water.

At the Mill Dam jetty, a reception party was waiting to escort them into the River Police Headquarters. MacDonald, Potts and several other senior officers watched incredulously as the casualties were brought ashore.

MacDonald's first comment just about summed up the whole adventure. 'Potts, man, you'd better cancel that Black Maria and call an ambulance!'

At two o'clock that morning, Jimmy Grainger sat huddled in the Bolams' lounge, drinking whisky and hot water. He wore his boss's dressing gown whilst Alec rummaged upstairs for a set of underclothing and a suit to replace Jimmy's own saturated outfit.

'Very good of you, Mrs Bolam, to take all this trouble!' he said, crouching thankfully over the fire. The icy waters of the Tyne's entrance still seemed to be in his bones and his teeth had only just stopped chattering.

Vera answered with a flippant brusqueness. 'I'm used to young folk cluttering the place up half the night!'

She felt surprised at her own pleasure at the opportunity to fuss over someone. It was years since Betty had been young enough to coddle and she had always been an independent, distant child.

Betty sat opposite now, upright and rather prim.

Bolam's voice came down the stairs, yelling, 'Vera, where the hell can I find some underpants for him?'

His wife sighed and went out, leaving the young people alone. There was a long silence, not an awkward one as far as Jimmy was concerned. He began to feel dozy and contented with the whisky and the fire and the success of the night.

'I'm sorry I slapped your face, Jimmy,' said Betty suddenly.

He grinned at her. 'Aw, forget it … it was nothing compared to the punch old Joe Blunt gave me tonight.' He touched his elbow gingerly. 'I should have let the old devil drown, but he sounded so pathetic when we fell into the drink – yelling for his mother. Couldn't swim a damn stroke!'

Betty loosened up a little. 'Must have been awful – what will happen to them now?'

'Life for Jackie Stott – which means about ten years in the nick, I suppose. Don't know what Joe will get, but with his record of violence, he can't expect to get much less.'

Alec and Vera came back into the room, laden with clothes.

'We're about the same size, Jimmy, these'll do till you get home.'

Bolam sounded almost too hearty and Vera looked at him sharply.

'You can't go mucking about in that bachelor hovel of yours, still soaked to the skin,' he continued. 'You want to get yourself married off, if you're going to make this midnight swimming a regular thing.'

Alec said this without a flicker of his eyes towards Betty. Grainger stood up.

'Thanks a lot – what's the drill for tomorrow – today, really?' he asked, looking at the clock.

'A special court at ten thirty – get Joe and Jackie remanded in custody. Abel Lupin won't be able to talk them out of this one!' he added with satisfaction. 'I heard on the way back that Hansen is improving a lot, so with luck we'll have him giving evidence before long – that'll really put the mockers on our two pals!'

Vera looked from one to the other. 'Will Hansen be charged with anything?'

Bolam shrugged. 'Probably – up to the DPP, but he was in pretty deep with Papagos and Casella. He's been concealing evidence about a murder and involved in a conspiracy to obtain money by menaces … I reckon he's for it!'

Alec's wife was interested in all the intrigues, though she normally avoided giving her husband the satisfaction of knowing it. 'What about the woman, this Laura Levine?'

'I don't know if they'll "do" her for anything – she concealed knowledge of Geordie's murder for a short time, but I can't see the DPP flogging himself over that charge.'

Jimmy clutched his dressing gown around him decorously. 'It's those two crooks from London that worry me … they're such a slippery pair. We've no guarantee that Hansen will drop them in it when he recovers. He might deny all Laura said! Those two yobs are powerful enough to terrorize him in or out of prison, even if they're doing a stretch themselves.'

Bolam nodded in unhappy agreement. 'MacDonald's afraid of that too – when Hansen wakes up, he's going to be in a terrible dilemma – either spill all the beans in the hope of getting a light sentence and then wait to be pushed under a bus by one of Papagos's boys – or keep his mouth shut and have the book thrown at him by the DPP and the trial judge!'

'Serve him bloody well right!' growled Jimmy and went upstairs to change into the dry clothes.

Vera went into the kitchen to look for some shoes for him.

Betty Bolam studied her fingernails carefully.

'And what will happen to Freddie Robson?' she murmured so quietly that her father could hardly hear her. 'Is he still locked up?'

To her surprise, Alec gave a chuckle and patted her shoulder. 'As far as I know, pet, he's sitting in his squalid bedsitter and has been since we left there this afternoon.'

Betty stared at him, wide-eyed. 'But Jimmy took him off to be charged with abduction!'

Bolam gave a deep belly laugh this time. 'Like blazes – he took him around the corner and gave him a good shaking and the best talking-to he's ever had in his life! Threatened him with prosecution of abduction, corruption, conspiracy and drug trafficking … none of which we had either the right or the evidence to pin on him!'

His voice hardened. 'Don't think it's not serious, Betty – it is! But if Freddie comes around here asking for you, you can have him! I say that because I know he damn well won't … and if he should, I sincerely hope that Jimmy Grainger isn't around. I'd hate to have to arrest my own sergeant for manslaughter!'

Betty listened to the sound of big feet tramping down the stairs and said nothing.

The Sixties Mysteries
by
Bernard Knight

The Lately Deceased
The Thread of Evidence
Mistress Murder
Russian Roulette
Policeman's Progress
Tiger at Bay
The Expert

For more information about **Bernard Knight**
and other **Accent Press** titles
please visit

www.accentpress.co.uk

CPSIA information can be obtained
at www.ICGtesting.com
Printed in the USA
LVOW12s2016010916

502845LV00001B/17/P